Robotworld

J.J. GARDNER

SCHOLASTIC INC.
New York Toronto London Auckland Sydney

No part of this publication may be reproduced in whole or in part, or stored in a retrieval system, or transmitted in any form or by any means, electronic, mechanical, photocopying, recording, or otherwise, without written permission of the publisher. For information regarding permission, write to Scholastic Inc., Attention: Permissions Department, 555 Broadway, New York, NY 10012.

ISBN 0-590-18938-7

12 11 10 9 8 7 6 5 4 3 2 1   8 9/9 0 1 2 3/0

Printed in the U.S.A.
First Scholastic printing, July 1998

1
A Midnight Snack

Pizza, thought Will Robinson. *What I wouldn't give for a slice of pepperoni pizza*. The only problem was the nearest pizza place was billions of light-years away. Back on Earth. Back home.

Will sighed and climbed out of his bunk. He rubbed his growling stomach. He had to eat something. Thoughts of raiding the ship's galley crossed his mind, but he quickly thought better of it. That was one of his dad's steadfast rules. Nobody eats after midnight. It was the only way to preserve the ship's food supply. At least until the family could find some environmentally friendly planet to set down on. Then there would be a few months of harvesting, some fuel regeneration, and Will and his family would blast off again and continue on to — where?

Will pressed a button on the wall and a small viewport beside his bed slid open. Though he saw nothing through it but the blackness of outer space his imagination saw something else. It saw a small world made mostly of blue and green water: Earth. Somewhere out there was Earth, the home he once knew. But for him and his family, finding Earth was like

1

finding a needle in a haystack. It had been only a few months, Earth time, since they blasted off from Houston Space Command in their spaceship, the *Jupiter 2*. A year since the mission to colonize a far off world called Alpha Prime began. And a year since the mission was sabotaged by the stowaway, Dr. Zachary Smith, causing the *Jupiter 2* to hurtle aimlessly into uncharted space.

Now they were hopelessly lost, each course change, each jump into hyperspace just a calculated gamble that may or may not take them closer to home.

And, for Will, closer to a slice of pepperoni pizza.

Suddenly, Will thought he saw something through the viewport. He blinked his eyes a few times and squinted. There *was* something out there. A small, distant speck of light that seemed no larger than a moth hole in an old sweater. Will wondered what it could be. Was it a star light-years away, whose ancient light was just now reaching his eyes? Or was it a planet, only miles away? If it was, it might be the perfect place to land the *Jupiter 2* and replenish its food and fuel supplies!

Will's heart began to pound with excitement. He even forgot about the grumbling in his stomach. He threw on his robe and raced out of his room. If there was a planet out there, he would know soon enough.

As Will took the turbolift to the upper deck of the *Jupiter 2*, he thought of waking his mom and dad. Or even the ship's pilot, Major West. But then he thought better of it. After all, what if the light out in space *was* only a star? There was no point in sounding a false alarm. There had been too many of those in the past.

Besides, though only ten years old, Will was the unofficial ensign aboard the ship. His job was Robotics, making certain that the mobile equipment aboard the *Jupiter 2* was in top working order. If the light out there was a planet, then it was his job to launch a working probe to investigate it.

"Hi, Robot!" said Will as he climbed out of the turbolift. The ship's Robot was standing on the main deck monitoring all the different computers that kept the ship running while the crew slept.

"Will Robinson, what are you doing here?" asked the Robot as it whirled to face him.

"Don't you see it, Robot?" said Will, pointing through the large viewscreen that was positioned directly over the main control console. "That light out there."

"A Robot does not 'see,' Will Robinson," replied the mechanical man matter-of-factly. "'Detect' would be a more correct term."

Will sighed. He often forgot that even though the Robot could talk like a human being, it was still only a mobile computer unit. And even though he had once saved the Robot's life by implanting his own personality engrams into its neural net, its view of the world was mostly as black and white as the logic board in his PC.

"All right, then, Robot," said Will. "Do you *detect* that light out there?"

"Affirmative, Will Robinson," replied the Robot.

"Have you been able to analyze it?"

"Affirmative. It is a planet orbiting exactly six-thousand-seven-hundred-thirty-three-point-five-miles away from its sun."

"A planet!" exclaimed Will excitedly. It was just what he had hoped for. "Is it inhabited? Is the air breathable? Is it safe to land there?"

"The planet is too far away for an environmental analysis," said the Robot. "And our course is not calibrated to take us any closer."

Will quickly slid into his seat behind the main robotics computer. He turned on the computer and quickly punched in his password. "Then I've got to act fast," he said. He entered a complicated sequence of commands. "I'm sending out a probe to the planet."

The Robot raised its oval-shaped head in alarm. "Warning, Will Robinson," it said. "You are not permitted to establish communications with unknown space bodies unless supervised by an adult."

"Come on, Robot. It's too late to wake Mom and Dad now," insisted Will. "Besides, like you said, we're moving away from the planet. I'll launch the probe, and if there's just a chance we can land there then I'll wake Mom and Dad. They'll know what to do."

Will entered one final command on the keyboard in front of him. "There," he said. "Probe launched."

"The probe will reach the planet in approximately five-minutes-and-forty-seven-seconds," announced the Robot.

"Then we wait," said Will and stared out through the viewport.

Although he did hope the planet responded to his signal, he couldn't help wondering what his dad would say when he found out Will had broken one of his rules. There was no way his dad was going to be happy about it, no matter what the outcome.

Suddenly the familiar grumbling of hunger returned in his stomach. "How much time did you say before the probe reaches the planet, Robot?"

"Currently the wait is five-point-thirty-six minutes and counting, Will Robinson," replied the Robot.

"How long before the probe starts sending back information?"

A series of whirs and hums sounded from the Robot's breastplate as it calculated the answer. "At our present speed, anywhere from ten to thirty minutes after contact."

Will couldn't wait that long. "I'm getting kind of hungry," he told the Robot. "Let's go to the galley and get something to eat."

"Warning, Will Robinson. That is breaking another one of your father's rules," the Robot informed Will.

Will sighed. "I guess you're right." He tried to force down his hunger. "But there's still some of that ice cream left over from tonight's dessert."

The Robot popped up its head. "Ice cream?"

"Yeah. With rainbow sprinkles."

"Ice cream! Yes! We must go for it, Will Robinson!" exclaimed the Robot. Then he added quizzically: "Why did I say that?"

"Because you're the coolest Robot ever!" burst out Will, a broad smile exploding across his face. "Last one to the galley is a dead asteroid!"

Will raced the Robot to the turbolift and down to the galley.

By the time the Robot reached the lower level, Will had already scooped out what was left of his mom's homemade pistachio ice cream and covered it with sprinkles. He had just swallowed the first cool, satisfying spoonful when he heard the whoosh of a door sliding open.

"Will Robinson!" he heard the familiar voice of his mother announce. "I thought I heard someone out here!"

Will cringed, his next spoonful of ice cream frozen somewhere between the bowl and his mouth. Maureen Robinson stood at the entrance of the galley area with a look of stern disapproval on her face.

"Will, you know you're not supposed to be in the galley after bedtime," said Mrs. Robinson. "And that ice cream was supposed to last us until tomorrow."

"Sorry, Mom. I couldn't sleep and I was just *so* hungry," said Will, knowing full well there was no excuse in the galaxy that would get him off the hook.

"Mrs. Robinson," the Robot jumped in. "I must take full responsibility for young Will's actions. I am programmed to enforce the ship's rules. I failed."

A suspicious look came over his mother's face. "You boys are like two mischievous brothers," she said. Then she grinned. "Lucky for you I'm not angry."

"You're not?" Will smiled.

"No," admitted Mrs. Robinson. "In fact, I couldn't sleep myself and thought I'd come out for a glass of warm milk. Now hurry up and finish what's left in that bowl and get back to bed."

"This does not compute, Mrs. Robinson," said the Robot.

"What's that, Robot?" asked Will's mom as she placed a glass of milk into the ship's thermowave heater.

"Will has broken a rule. I have failed in my duty. It is only logical that we must pay for our crime. Instead, you are allowing Will to finish his ice cream and you are not shutting my power off."

"That's true," said Mrs. Robinson. "Robot, you will learn by living with us humans that we are not always logical. In fact, we can be downright illogical. You see, sometimes there are things we feel helpless to control. Craving food can be one of

6

them. Even I couldn't resist a midnight snack. And as for shutting your power down, well — I forgive you, too."

"Forgive?" the Robot repeated the word. "It does not compute."

"Will," began Mrs. Robinson. "You understand what you did was wrong, don't you?"

"Yes, ma'am," replied Will. "I'll go without dessert tomorrow, if it's all right with you."

Mrs. Robinson smiled proudly at Will. She was just about to reply when a loud alarm sounded from the upper deck.

"What on Earth could have set that off?" she asked.

But Will knew perfectly well what it was. "The probe!" he exclaimed. "We're getting a signal from that planet!"

2
The Signal

"Planet?" Maureen Robinson repeated. "What planet?"

"There's no time to explain now!" replied Will. Without another word he raced into the turbolift and headed to the upper deck.

It wasn't long before the others aboard the *Jupiter 2* had been roused by the sound of the alarm.

"Will, what's this about a planet?" asked his father, Professor John Robinson, as he and Mrs. Robinson joined Will at the command console. By now Will had turned off the alarm while the Robot quickly began analyzing data that was being transmitted back from the probe.

"I couldn't sleep and I thought I saw something through my viewport," Will said, quickly bringing his father up to date. "It turned out to be a planet so I launched a probe."

"Who gave you permission to launch a probe, son?" asked Professor Robinson.

Will lowered his eyes, but there was no time to answer. Soon everyone had arrived on the upper deck.

"What's going on?" asked Major Don West, the ship's

rugged-looking pilot. He immediately sat in one of the command seats and began checking the ship's navigational instruments. "Are we still on course?"

"Something woke us up," said Will's older sister, Penny. In her arms was Blawp, her brightly colored monkeylike alien pet. "And Blawp freaked."

"I thought I heard an alarm go off," said Will's oldest sister, Judy. "Is everyone all right?"

"So that *was* an alarm," came the voice of Dr. Smith. He seemed the most disturbed of everybody. "Are we under attack? I don't see any alien battleships. Have we found Earth?"

"Everybody relax," said Professor Robinson. "We've just received a signal from a nearby planet, that's all."

"A planet?" asked Judy. "Is it habitable, Dad?"

"Doesn't make a difference if it is," said Major West as he checked the gyroscope. "It's way too far away from our present trajectory for us to change course and land on it."

"Thank heavens for that," said Dr. Smith. "I for one have no interest in spending any time on some desolate lump of rock when Earth could be just around the next corner."

"Dr. Smith, that does not compute," interjected the Robot. "There are no corners in space. Space is defined as the infinite extension of the three-dimensional field in which all matter exists —"

"Spare me your unimaginative analysis," Smith shot back through an uncontrollable yawn. "I'm tired and it was a figure of speech."

The Robot twirled one of its antennae, almost as if it were offended by Dr. Smith's comment.

"Environmental analysis of the planet is now complete," the

Robot suddenly announced. "Do you wish to hear the data, Professor Robinson?"

"Negative, Robot," replied Professor Robinson, much to Will's surprise. "However, you can supply a printout of the information to me in the morning."

"Understood, Professor," said the Robot obediently.

"But, Dad —!" Will started, wondering why his father did not want to learn more about the planet.

"Now I want everyone to return to bed," Professor Robinson said, ignoring Will. "We all have to be at our most alert tomorrow for our next jump into hyperspace."

Once everyone began to head back to the turbolift, Professor Robinson said, "Will, you stay up here a minute."

Uh-oh, thought Will, a shiver traveling down to his toes. It was lecture time, and if Will knew his father, it was going to be a serious one.

"Will, you never answered my question," Professor Robinson said when only he, Will, Will's mother, and the Robot were left on the upper deck. "Who gave you permission to send a probe to that planet?"

"No one, sir," admitted Will. "I just thought —"

"You just thought you'd investigate —" started his father.

"Yeah!" agreed Will with enthusiasm.

"— and jeopardize the safety of everyone aboard the *Jupiter 2*," Professor Robinson finished. "Look, Will, suppose there was an alien race on that planet who didn't like the idea of a strange probe invading them? Or suppose some other part of the ship's computers became unbalanced when you launched the probe?"

"But the *planet* —" insisted Will.

"Will, we are going to find lots of planets on our travels," said his mom. "But the *Jupiter 2* is a highly sensitive piece of equipment. Just because we see a planet doesn't mean we should change our course in midstream, even if it's the most perfect planet in the universe."

"And if the Robot thought that there was time to investigate that planet and recalibrate our course then he would have awoken us," added Will's dad. "That's why we have him monitor the helm while we sleep. That's one of his jobs."

Will remained silent. He knew his father was right. He realized now that he had risked the lives of his family and everyone else by launching that probe.

"You're right, sir," he admitted. "I guess I wasn't thinking."

"I guess you weren't," agreed his father. "You're going to have to be punished for this mistake, Will. Tomorrow your mother and I will decide what that punishment will be. Understand?"

"Yes, sir," said Will, realizing there was a big difference between doing something for yourself and putting others in danger. He silently promised himself to think before he acted in the future.

"Now off to bed with you," ordered his dad.

"Good night, Mom," said Will, giving his mother a gentle kiss on her cheek. "Good night, Dad."

Will's parents said good night.

"Good night, Robot," said Will.

The Robot swerved toward Will. But instead of returning his good night, it suddenly jerked its dome-topped head to alertness in a familiar way. Will and his parents knew something was wrong.

"Warning! Warning!" the robot announced in a tone that sent a chill down Will's spine. "Warning! Warning!"

11

"What's wrong, Robot?" asked Will, rushing over to his friend. He waited for an explanation.

But to Will's surprise, Robot did not explain. "Warning! Warning!" it repeated. Now it was waving its arms frantically. *"Danger! Danger!"*

3
Hijacked!

"Robot, what's wrong?" Will asked again.

"Danger! Danger!" the Robot continued to cry.

"Robot," demanded Will's father. "What's the reason for this alert?"

The Robot gave no answer. Instead, it suddenly stopped waving its arms and became silent.

"Robot?" asked Will, becoming concerned. "Are you okay?"

But the Robot still would not answer. Will looked at his parents uneasily.

"What's wrong with him, Dad?" Will asked.

"I don't know, son," replied Professor Robinson. "But I think we'd better remove his power pack. We'll have to do a complete diagnostic on him tomorrow."

"But, Dad —!"

"I know how you feel son," said Will's dad. "But, remember our agreement?"

Will remembered the agreement and shuddered. Soon after taking off from Earth, the Robot had been operating under orders from Dr. Smith to destroy the *Jupiter 2*. After getting the Robot under control, his dad had let Will overhaul the Robot.

Later, the Robot had been almost completely destroyed while protecting the crew from giant alien spiders. Will had to rebuild the Robot practically from scratch. Now it was Will's job to make absolutely certain the Robot functioned properly. At the first sign of any malfunction it was agreed that Will would shut the Robot down — for good, if necessary.

It was not something Will ever thought he would have to do.

"Let me do it, Dad," said Will. "Sorry about this, Robot." He reached forward to pull the power pack off of the Robot's metallic shell. As he did, the Robot swung his huge arm and sent Will flying several yards across the deck.

"Will!" shouted his mother as she ran to help him to his feet. "Will, are you all right?"

Will was fine, at least on the outside. Inside, it was another matter. He couldn't imagine what had made the Robot slug him.

"Robot," he said, starting toward the mechanical man. "Why did you —?"

"Stay back, Will," said Professor Robinson, who was dodging toward the Robot in another attempt to remove its power pack.

"John, be careful!" warned Mrs. Robinson.

But it was too late. The Robot extended its arm and let out a laser blast that sent John hurtling to the floor, stunned. Will and his mom ran to help his dad.

Next, the Robot moved to the main command center. There he began inputting new commands into one of the control keyboards. Will recognized the keyboard immediately as the one that patched into the ship's navigational computer.

"Robot, stop!" shouted Will. "I order you to stop!"

But instead of obeying Will, the Robot speeded up its entries. Gradually, power from the ship's thruster engines could be felt swelling through the floor. Then the ship suddenly heaved at such an angle that Will and his mother lost their balance and were thrown to the floor.

"Dad, what's happening?!" shouted Will. "I can't move! My legs feel like they weigh a ton!"

The force of the new and unusually slanted angle of the ship had both Will and his parents pinned to the floor.

"It's g-force!" Will's dad shouted back a reply. "The pressure of gravity!"

"That means the ship is changing direction!" exclaimed Maureen.

"That's right . . ." said Professor Robinson, the g-force against his face making it difficult to speak. "Robot . . . changed . . . trajectory but forgot . . . to compensate for . . . change in velocity! Must compensate for gravity pressure . . . or we'll be crushed!"

Suddenly the *Jupiter 2* began to level off. The pressure that had pinned Will and his parents to the ground lifted. A moment later Will saw Don West climbing up on deck from the ladder that connected the upper and lower levels of the ship. A laser pistol was in his hand. Without warning, Major West aimed and fired at the Robot, hitting the power pack squarely. The power pack exploded and the Robot slumped over, deactivated.

"Robot!" cried Will as he ran to its side.

"Everybody all right?" asked Major West.

"Yes, fine," replied Mrs. Robinson. "What happened?"

"I thought I'd do a quick systems check in the back-up computer drive down below before going back to bed," explained Major West. "Before I knew it I felt the change in gravity pressure. Fortunately I was able to override the effect and

15

compensate for the change in velocity. What happened up here?"

"The Robot went berserk again," answered Professor Robinson.

"I'll bet Smith had something to do with it," Major West snarled.

"I beg your pardon, Major!" came the indignant voice of Dr. Smith from behind. He, Judy, and Penny had now joined the others topside. "But I had nothing to do with it!"

"Why is it whatever you say makes me believe just the opposite?" Major West asked Smith doubtfully.

"I'll remind you, Major," huffed Smith, "that I am trapped out here in cosmic oblivion with the rest of you. Why would I risk my own life as well?"

"I don't know, Smith," Major West shot back. "But I'm sure you'd have a good reason."

"That's enough, both of you," ordered Professor Robinson.

"Dad, the Robot doesn't seem to be too damaged," said Will. In his hand was the shattered power pack. "But this power pack is beyond repair."

"Let's worry about the Robot later, son," said his father. "Right now we've got to get back on course."

"That's going to be a bit of a problem," said Major West, who had already begun to evaluate the new course the Robot had laid in. "The Robot created a subprogram in the navigation system that won't let me override its course change no matter what I try."

"Where are we headed?" asked Judy.

"Take a look," said Major West, pointing at the viewport.

"It's the planet I sent the probe to!" exclaimed Will, stunned. They were now drawing closer to the planet with each passing second.

"We're going to crash!" announced Smith with alarm.

"Relax, Smith," said Don. "The Robot programmed us for a soft landing."

"Land? Where?" asked Penny.

"The Robot took care of that, too," said Don, reading the data from his computer. "Picked out a plum spot for us to set down."

"Do we even know what's down there?" asked Judy.

Mrs. Robinson quickly took her seat at the life sciences station. "I'm analyzing data from that probe: atmospheric and environmental conditions able to sustain human life. There's vegetation and water and — that's odd!"

"What is it, Maureen?" asked John.

"There are cities on several continents, but no people."

"What's so strange about that?" remarked Dr. Smith. "No doubt the remnants of some unfortunate extinct alien race."

"That may be so Dr. Smith," said Mrs. Robinson. "But everything in those cities — every building, every public utility — right down to the last electrical surge, is in full operation!"

4
Welcoming Committee

"It'll be about five minutes before we enter the planet's orbit," announced Don.

"I want everybody strapped in, pronto," ordered Professor Robinson. "Looks like we're going in for a landing."

Dr. Smith groaned loudly, unhappily joining the others as they climbed into the ship's landing seats and strapped themselves in.

Will was the last to strap in. The Robot had needed to be secured before landing and that was part of his job. He did it by using the remote control relay at his robotics computer. A special radio signal controlled the Robot's movements without activating it. Within minutes Will was magnetically locking the Robot into its specially designed stasis chamber. When he was done he looked at the Robot sadly.

"I know you can't hear me, Robot," he said. "But when this is all over I'm gonna find out what went wrong with you and I'm gonna fix you. I promise."

Will climbed into his landing seat.

"Gee, Will, that was good thinking launching a valuable

18

space probe to a planet while we're moving away from it at top speed," said Penny from the next seat, a taunting lilt in her voice. "What were you trying to do? Earn a promotion to captain or something?"

Blawp, its leathery-skinned arms wrapped securely around Penny's chest, let out a couple of snickering snorts.

"I think the two of you have been breathing in too much artificial oxygen," Will shot back.

"Oh, listen to the brave astronaut," said Penny. "Don't get mad at me because you messed up."

Will wanted to stick up for himself, but somehow thought better of it. Now, he knew, was not the best time to get into an argument with his sister. Besides, Penny was right. Not only had he gotten himself into trouble, but he felt responsible for what had gone wrong with the Robot as well.

"I guess you're right," he admitted to his sister. "I deserve whatever I've got coming to me."

Penny seemed slightly startled by her brother's honesty. "I'm sorry, Will," she apologized. "We're lost in space, trapped in this hunk of metal billions of miles from everything that once meant something to us. I guess there's no punishment Dad or anyone else can come up with that could be worse than that."

Will looked up at his sister and smiled, comforted by her words.

"Entering planet's orbit," Major West announced from the helm. "Contact with the planet's surface minus twelve minutes and counting. . . ."

Will glanced over at the command console where his father and Major West sat operating the many controls that would guide the huge *Jupiter 2* down to the planet. Even though the

Robot had preprogrammed the ship to land, it still took a complicated series of checks and double-checks to make sure everything went smoothly.

Glancing further up he could see the planet growing larger in the helm viewport. By now they had descended so close it completely filled the wide window. Will noticed that the planet didn't look all that different from Earth. There seemed to be several large bodies of water that were broken up by continents of all different shapes and sizes. Clouds covered the planet and were clearly more dense in some spots than others. What made this world different from Earth, Will noticed, was that the water looked more red than blue and the clouds looked more green than white. These peculiar features didn't surprise him. Many of the worlds he and his family visited in space had one unusual environmental characteristic or another, the result of many different factors such as the distance from their suns or radiation levels in their atmospheres.

"Touchdown minus eight minutes and counting. . . ." Will heard Major West continue the countdown. "Main retros coming on line!"

Just then the ship's retro engines began to power up. Their low hum could be heard throughout the ship. Although the engines were decks below them, Will and the others could easily feel their rumble.

Now Will could see that the *Jupiter 2* was passing through a green mist, obviously a layer of the planet's strangely colored clouds. Within minutes the mist faded and the first recognizable sign of civilization could be seen. Will and the others nearly gasped at the sight. It was a city, as big and complex as any they had known on Earth, a vast mixture of buildings and walkways, roads, and highways.

At a speed close to nine hundred miles per hour, the *Jupiter*

2 soared across the tops of the tallest buildings of the alien city. It seemed to be headed for a destination somewhere beyond them.

"T minus three minutes and counting. . . ." Major West said now.

Just then Will felt the ship slow down, almost as if it were coming to a full stop. He knew at once that the ship's landing rockets had come on. Next, he felt his body press deep into his landing seat as the angle of the ship changed from a downward slope to a more level one. Through the viewport he saw the buildings of the planet's city slip from view, replaced by nothing but the pinkish alien sky. This meant the ship had taken a position parallel to the surface below and its main landing supports were most certainly descending from their hatches. It would be less than a minute now before they would touch down.

"This is it!" said Will's dad. "Everyone a-okay back there?"

Everyone either nodded or replied with a "roger." Months of pre-flight training back on Earth had prepared the Robinsons for the routine of a basic touchdown.

"Twelve seconds," they heard Major West call out the final countdown. "Eleven seconds . . . ten seconds . . . nine . . . eight . . ."

Seven . . . six . . . five . . . Will counted silently to himself as the seconds to landing swiftly ticked by. *Four . . . three . . . two . . . one!*

There was a soft jolt as the ship touched down. Almost instantly its many engines began to whir to a stop. They had landed safely. Now Will looked over and saw his mother's shoulders relax as she let out a sigh of relief. Everyone else seemed relieved as well. One by one they unstrapped themselves from their landing seats and joined Major West and

Professor Robinson at the helm. Everyone wanted to get a closer look at this new world they had landed on.

But when they reached the front of the ship they were startled by their first view of the planet. They were far from the city, perhaps twenty miles or so. The land directly around them was like a desert. And something was coming toward them. From the look of it, it seemed to be a large crowd.

"I thought there weren't any life-forms on this planet, Mom," said Penny as she watched the crowd move closer to the ship.

"It could be a life-form our ship's computers couldn't recognize," Will reasoned aloud.

"There are certainly a lot of them, aren't there?" said Dr. Smith, watching the crowd nervously. "You don't suppose they're hostile, do you?"

"We can't know what their intentions are yet, Dr. Smith," said Professor Robinson.

"Then I suggest we all arm ourselves, just in case," said Smith. He headed to an arsenal compartment.

"Stay away from there, Smith," ordered Major West. "No one takes a weapon without Professor Robinson's okay."

"Are you out of your mind, Major," said Dr. Smith, the panic in his voice becoming more intense. "Why, look at the size of that crowd. There must be hundreds ... *thousands* of them! We need some sort of protection."

"The doctor's got a point," said Professor Robinson. "Don, activate the force field."

"Roger," said Major West. He flicked a switch. A second later the computer confirmed that the ship was protected by its invisible force field.

By then the crowd had gotten so close that it was now possible to make out individual characteristics among them.

"They look like they're made out of metal," observed Will.

"They *are* metallic in nature, John," announced Mrs. Robinson, who had quickly checked the sensors at her Life Sciences stations. "In fact, according to our sensors they're . . . *machines*."

"Robots?" questioned Judy.

"Maybe they're just a welcoming committee," quipped Major West.

"Look," said Penny. "They're stopping."

The crowd of robots had now come to a stop about two hundred yards from the ship. It had to. That was about the range that the *Jupiter 2*'s force field could reach. For a long moment everyone was silent while they stared at the crowd. The robots were as varied from one another as a hundred different species of plant or animal life. There were tall ones, short ones, wide ones, thin ones. Some were of complex designs with a myriad of tiny components, while others looked as smooth and simple as tin cans or metal beach balls.

"Why doesn't one of them try to contact us?" asked Penny.

Then, almost as if in answer to her question, the robots began to move forward again. As soon as they did, they came in contact with the ship's force field, causing a great electrical surge of lightning and sparks.

But the force field didn't stop them. One by one the robots passed through it as easily as if it were made of air. Now they were moving closer to the *Jupiter 2*.

"They broke through!" shouted Smith. "They're going to kill us all!"

5
The Monster Machine

"Look!" exclaimed Will. "They've stopped again!"

The robots had not attacked the ship as Dr. Smith had predicted. Instead, after passing unobstructed through the *Jupiter 2*'s force field, they came to a complete stop only inches away from the viewport.

As soon as they stopped their advance, a loud, high-pitched sound suddenly pierced the ship. It was so loud that Will and the others had to cover their ears.

"What is *that*?" shrieked Penny.

The sound seemed to have an effect on the strange robots outside. They began to move away from each other, parting until a narrow passageway had been created between them. Through the passageway a monstrous figure could be seen. It was a machine that towered over all the rest. And it was heading right toward the *Jupiter 2*.

The monster machine must have been nearly twelve feet tall. Its body was shaped like a triangle. It looked like a flying pyramid with all sorts of controls and flashing lights on it. Its enormous head was round and spiked like a star. With long gray metallic arms that jutted from its sides, it wildly waved a pair of deadly-looking claws as it menacingly made its way down the narrow path. It stopped in front of the *Jupiter 2*.

"That one seems to have some kind of control over the other robots," noticed Judy.

"It could have some kind of built-in remote control mechanism," theorized Will.

"Perhaps it is the leader here," guessed Dr. Smith.

"I'm going to try and communicate with it," said Professor Robinson. He walked over to the ship's communication station. "This is Professor John Robinson, Commander of the *Jupiter 2*," Will's dad said, speaking through the ship's communicator. "We're travelers lost in space. We were forced to land on your planet due to a malfunction in our ship's Robot."

No one could be sure if the strange alien machine understood Professor Robinson's message. It raised one of its arms and aimed it directly at the viewport. The high-pitched shrill sound filled the ship again.

Suddenly, the power bands that braced the Robot in its stasis chamber began to hum with magnetic power. Then the Robot's breastplate lit up. The Robot became activated and straightened itself to alertness.

"It must be using that device to patch into the Robot's internal power supply!" Will shouted excitedly. He ran to the Robot. "Robot, can you hear me?"

"Yes," replied the Robot weakly. "I can hear you, Will Robinson."

"Robot, can you explain any of this?" interjected Professor Robinson.

"Yeah, why did you land us here?" asked Major West.

"What do those machines out there want?" asked Mrs. Robinson.

"They want — *me* — Mrs. Robinson," replied the Robot.

Just then the huge monster machine outside let out another high-pitched signal. At the sound, the Robot started out of its stasis chamber and headed for the main inner hatch.

"Make way," demanded the Robot. "I am being summoned."

"Robot, where are you going?" asked Will. "Robot, stop! I order you to stop!"

"I cannot, Will Robinson," replied the Robot. "My internal computers have been taken over by others. My actions are no longer under my control."

"Who's controlling them, Robot?"

"*They* are," the Robot replied, pointing to the robots outside. "Now move aside."

The Robot reached over and pressed the inner hatch release. But the hatch did not open. Major West had managed to override it through the helm computer.

"What have you done, Major?" asked Dr. Smith. "Can't you see those things out there want our Robot? Give it to them and maybe they'll let us alone!"

"No, Dr. Smith," insisted Will. "He's our Robot. And he's my friend!"

"We're leaving here with every member of our crew, Dr. Smith," Professor Robinson told Dr. Smith defiantly, "including our Robot."

Will beamed at his father's words.

"Are you mad, Robinson?" said Dr. Smith. "There's an army of them out there. They may destroy us if we don't let them have what they want. What I'm suggesting is called 'survival of the fittest.'"

"Don't listen to him, Dad!" said Will. "Dr. Smith, how'd you like it if we left you here all alone, huh?"

"We're not leaving anybody behind, Will," said his dad. "Don, how long before we can regain control of the ship?"

"I'll start working on it right away," said Major West. "Let's go, Smith."

"Go? Where?" replied Dr. Smith.

"Below deck to try and purge the main computer drive," replied Major West. "I'll need some help."

"Major West, I'm a doctor who served in the millennial wars," Dr. Smith said, offended, "not a computer programmer."

"You're a weasel, Smith," Major West shot back. "Now let's get going. Or maybe Will has a point. We can always offer you to that monster machine out there in exchange for our freedom."

"Just try it, Major," challenged Dr. Smith.

From his tense body language everyone could see that Major West would have liked nothing more than to make good on his threat. Instead, he restrained himself and headed to the turbolift, seemingly unconcerned if Smith followed him or not.

"Doctor," said Professor Robinson. "If you don't want to spend the rest of your trip with us locked up in the brig, I suggest you go and help Major West."

Smith could tell Professor Robinson meant what he said. He begrudgingly followed Major West down below.

"Dad! Look out!" shouted Judy a moment later.

The monster machine had just let out another signal. Now the Robot turned away from the main inner hatch and moved toward the helm.

"I am being summoned!" he said. "Out of my way, Professor Robinson!"

The Robot pushed past Professor Robinson and began inputting new commands into the helm computer. Professor Robinson ordered the Robot to stop, but the Robot would not pay attention. He tried grabbing the huge ball bearings that comprised the Robot's great arm, but the Robot flicked him aside as if he were a fly.

"Dad!" shouted Will as he and the others ran to his father's aid. Professor Robinson was nearly unconscious.

By now the Robot had returned to the hatch. He was about to open it when Will ran to the weapons station and quickly input the coordinates of the monster machine. The machine appeared on the vector screen. Will grasped his hands around the power sticks that controlled the ship's external lasers and skillfully zeroed in on the monster machine. Then he fired, his thumb pressing down hard on the laser stick's power button. A low voltage laser bolt shot out from the underbelly of the *Jupiter 2* and struck the monster machine dead center.

There was an explosion. Fire and sparks erupted from the machine as parts of it began to explode. Then its massive arms, which had just before been aimed at the *Jupiter 2*, went limp. The top half of its tall body hunched over and its huge round head slumped to the side.

Will had deactivated the machine.

"You did it, Will!" Penny exclaimed happily. "But look!"

Will and the others looked out through the viewport at the disabled monster. Something on it was moving. After a moment, a small door on its side opened. Then a ladder made of rope was thrown out. Next, a figure stepped out of the machine.

"It's a boy!" said Penny.

A boy, who looked no older than Penny, had emerged from inside the machine and was now trying to climb down its side. But it quickly became clear that the boy was weak, probably hurt by Will's laser blast. The boy barely made it down a few steps before he staggered dizzily.

Then he suddenly lost his footing and fell the rest of the way to the ground.

6
Alien Aboard

"All right, Robot," said Will. "Access your internal system files and begin reinitializing."

"Roger, Will Robinson," replied the Robot. The Robot let out an intense series of whirs, clicks, and beeps that told the young scientist it was obeying his command.

Nearly an hour had passed since the *Jupiter 2* had landed on the machine dominated alien planet. But in that hour, so much had happened. The ship had been confronted by an army of automatons. One of them, a mechanical monster, had tried to kidnap the Robot. Had Will not disabled it with one of the ship's external lasers the Robot might not be with him now.

He and the Robot were in the computer lab. Will was determined to find out what strange power the inhabitants of this planet seemed to have over his preprogrammed friend. He had decided to purge the Robot's main computer drive and rebuild it system by system until he found the problem.

But so far he was having no luck. Now, as the Robot began to noisily overhaul its system files, Will was becoming even more worried than before. If he couldn't find out what went wrong with the Robot, then how would he be able to protect it from the aliens?

He began to suspect that the secret lay with that alien boy, the one who tried to escape from inside the monster machine after Will had shot it. The boy was now in the ship's sickbay, unconscious, and under the care of Will's sister Judy. Will hoped the boy would survive and give them the answers he sought.

"How's it going, son?" Will heard a voice ask. It was his father, who, he realized, must have taken a break from helping Don and Dr. Smith get the ship back to full working order.

"It's hard to say," replied Will. "I've checked the Robot inside and out. I just can't find any sign of a virus."

"Have you checked for any corrupted downloaded subprograms?" asked Will's father helpfully. "How about checking its link-up with the ship's own ROM? Or checking for extensions conflicts?"

Will smiled. His dad was the top scientist in his field when it came to hyperdrive mechanics and subwarp interdimensional space flight. But when it came to electronics and Robotics, that was Will's specialty, and he knew as much as his dad did. In fact, he was so good at it his mom didn't have to include it in his daily tutoring sessions.

"I've checked out all that, Dad," Will told his father. "There's just no place else to look. Besides . . ."

"What is it, son?" asked Professor Robinson, noticing Will's hesitation.

"Well," began Will, thoughtfully. "I just can't shake this feeling that whatever's wrong with the Robot is coming from some outside source. And that that source isn't limited by the Robot's physical technology."

A quizzical look came over his father's face. "You mean the

Robot is being controlled by some kind of mental telepathy?" he asked. "That's impossible, at least where the Robot is concerned."

"Why?" asked Will.

"Will, I know you like to think of the Robot as a person, but don't forget he's not human. His brain is only a series of programs and sub-programs. In the end he's only a machine. And he's only as smart as what we put inside him. In any event, I'm sure we'll learn more when the alien boy revives."

Will paused. "Dad," he started. "I know this is all my fault. If I'd obeyed the rules and hadn't launched that probe, then the Robot probably never would have taken over the ship. We'd probably be safe on some more friendly planet by now."

"Sending the probe *was* wrong, Will," agreed his father. "But sometimes even I forget how much your scientific curiosity can get the better of you. No matter what happens, I'm still proud of you. We'll discuss rules and regulations later." Then he added with a smile, "Right now, keep working on that Robot!"

"Yes, sir!" Will said, smiling back.

Just then a call signal came over the ship's intercom. It was Judy.

"Dad," said Judy. "The alien's coming around!"

Will and his father quickly joined the others in sickbay. The alien boy was now sitting up in bed. This was the first good look Will had gotten of the boy since his father and mother took him inside. He was a little taller than Will, with strange pinkish-orange skin that seemed unbruised by his fall. His skin and head were very smooth and it didn't look to Will as if he had any hair at all. His body was very thin, not more than twelve or thirteen inches all around, giving him a frail appearance. His face was exceptionally delicate with a pair of eyes set vertically instead of horizontally in his face and ears that seemed to grow inward instead of outward. They looked like holes in the sides of his head. Dressed in a one-piece suit made of shimmering material with a round chestplate in the center, the boy looked almost human.

"He hasn't said a word since he came to," said Judy once her father had arrived. "He won't answer any of my questions, so I'm sure he doesn't speak any Earth language. He doesn't seem to be bruised or hurt — not on the outside, at least, but that doesn't surprise me."

"Why?" asked her father.

"Look at this," Judy said as she popped a disk into her medical computer. The computer monitor booted up, revealing a schematic of the boy's skeleton: a complex network of tiny, almost microscopic electronic units.

"He's an android!" exclaimed Will, who had read theoretical essays on androids back on Earth.

Suddenly the android boy slid off his bed. With an expression of curiosity, he looked everyone over. Then he began moving up to each person: Professor Robinson, Maureen, Judy, Don, and Dr. Smith. He studied each one for a long moment before moving on to the next. When he came to Penny he reached out and touched her black hair. Penny smiled shyly as he did this. Then he moved to Will.

He took Will's wrist and raised it, comparing Will's fingers to his own hands. Each boy had five fingers, but the android's were longer and much thinner. And his skin was so delicate Will could almost see right through it.

"My name is Will Robinson," Will told the android nervously. "I'm from Earth. You're on the *Jupiter 2* spaceship. We mean you no harm. I didn't mean to hurt you with our laser but I thought you were going to take our Robot."

The android opened his mouth to reply. But no sooner had he done so than the chestplate on his suit lit up with a pulsating light. This seemed to have some kind of mesmerizing control over the boy. He turned out of sickbay and headed toward the computer lab.

"He's heading for the Robot!" shouted Will with alarm. He and the others ran after the android boy. When they reached the computer lab the alien turned around to face them.

On the chestplate of the android's suit was a round knob. When he turned the knob, a ray shot out from its center and flooded the deck.

Suddenly everyone was surrounded by an invisible force field. The strength of the force field was so great no one was able to move or speak. All they could do was watch helplessly as the android boy walked up to the Robot.

They watched helplessly as the android turned the knob on its chestplate and emitted that strange high-pitched signal that seemed to have some kind of hypnotizing control over the Robot.

And they watched helplessly as the Robot followed the android out of the *Jupiter 2* and disappeared beyond view.

7
Inside the Monster Machine

As suddenly as it had started, the android's force field disappeared. Will and the others were soon able to move again.

"Dad, he's got the Robot!" cried Will as he ran to the viewport. But when he got there the android and the Robot were nowhere to be seen.

"It was a trick all along," suggested Dr. Smith. "That creature or whatever it was just wanted to get on board so he could steal the Robot."

"That was no trick," Judy told Dr. Smith. "The android was not functioning when we brought him on board, I'm sure of that."

"Well, he can't have gotten very far on foot," noted Major West, pointing outside. "His machine is still here."

Outside the ship, the android's monster machine remained in a state of disrepair.

"Let's arm up, Don," said Will's dad. "We'll take the chariot and go after them."

"John," said Mrs. Robinson in a concerned tone of voice. "Be careful."

"We will," said Professor Robinson. Then he took Mrs. Robinson aside and kissed her good-bye.

In a little while he and Major West grabbed a couple of laser pistols and lowered the chariot out of its hangar in the underbelly of the *Jupiter 2*. The chariot was a fully equipped army tank-sized vehicle with powerful tractor wheels and a protective titanium casing that was capable of withstanding all kinds of environmental dangers. Major West did a quick systems check to make sure the great mobile land rover was in working order. Everything checked out fine.

"I want everyone to stay inside the ship until we get back," Professor Robinson told the others. "Maureen, track us by radar. We'll radio in every thirty minutes."

"Good luck, Dad," Will said hopefully, as his father prepared to climb into the chariot.

Professor Robinson gave Will a thumbs-up. Then he and Major West disappeared from view. Within seconds the chariot was rolling off into the distance.

Mrs. Robinson began tracking the chariot's movements by radar as soon as it departed. Will, Penny, and Judy each took turns tracing the chariot's signal. It seemed like it took forever before the first thirty minutes passed by. Then, to everyone's relief Professor Robinson radioed in, just as he had promised. By now he and Major West were approaching the alien city. So far, however, there was no sign of the alien boy or the Robot.

The second thirty-minute interval passed just as slowly as the first. On the radar screen everyone could see that the chariot had come to a full stop. This time, however, there was no message from Professor Robinson or Major West.

"Give them another few minutes," Mrs. Robinson told the

children, trying to remain calm. "Perhaps they wandered away from the chariot."

But the minutes ticked by with no word from Professor Robinson or Major West. Something was wrong. Mrs. Robinson called to her husband over the communicator, but no matter how often she increased the range of her signal, he did not reply.

"I'm getting worried, Mom," said Judy.

"Me, too," said Will and Penny.

It didn't take long for Mrs. Robinson to decide what to do. "It may be nothing more than a faulty radio circuit," she said, thinking aloud. "But if we don't hear from them in an hour, I'm going to go look for them. And Dr. Smith, you're going with me."

"*I*, madam?" Dr. Smith replied nervously.

"That's right, *you*. Judy, may I speak with you?" Mrs. Robinson then took her eldest daughter aside.

Will had a feeling that something was up and if he knew anything about command procedure, then he knew what it was.

"Mom told you to take us and blast off if we don't hear from her or Dr. Smith when they go looking for Dad, didn't she?" he asked his oldest sister earnestly.

"Yes, Will," Judy admitted. "But don't worry. I'm sure we'll hear from Dad and Don."

Will looked out at the alien city that sat on the horizon and crossed his fingers. After a few minutes he felt someone standing behind him. It was Dr. Smith.

"Who knows what these alien savages have in mind for us," he wondered aloud to the boy.

"What do you mean, Dr. Smith?" asked Will.

"It's obvious they kidnapped your father and Major West as well as our Robot, isn't it?"

Will had tried not to think of it, but, in fact, that was exactly his fear. "I wish there was something we could do," he said.

"There *is* one thing," Dr. Smith started to suggest.

"What?"

"The alien android must have thought that mechanical monstrosity out there is broken beyond repair, otherwise he would have taken it when he left," said Dr. Smith. "We can repair it and return it to him."

"What good would that do?" asked Will.

"A gesture of good will is sometimes rewarded in kind," suggested Dr. Smith. "Their machine in exchange for our freedom."

"But Dad said to stay inside," insisted Will.

"Your father is not here now," said Smith. "And one can only imagine the danger he may be in. And now your mother stands a chance of putting herself right smack in the middle of it. Does that seem right to you when the answer to our problems may be right in front of us? Besides, you must admit that you are the one to blame for getting us into this situation."

Smith wanted nothing more than to save his own hide from having to go search for Will's father and Major West, Will knew. The only thing was that Smith was right. This whole mess *was* Will's fault. He would give anything to get his family out of danger.

"But I've never even seen a robot like that one," said Will with uncertainty.

"I'm sure someone with your technical expertise in electronics and robotics can get that thing working," Dr. Smith said in a persuasive tone of voice.

Will thought for a minute. "I suppose I could probably patch into some of its peripheral files with one of the ship's portable computer drives and a battery," he reasoned aloud.

"There you go, little professor!" exclaimed Dr. Smith quietly. "Now you're thinking like a true scientist!"

Mrs. Robinson was spending most of her time at the radar station now, her concentration focused on trying to locate Will's dad and Major West. Will knew it would be an easy matter for him and Dr. Smith to sneak out to the alien machine.

He grabbed some peripherals from the computer lab and threw them into a backpack. Then he flung the pack over his shoulder and took the turbolift down to the bottom deck of the *Jupiter 2*. To be on the safe side he grabbed a small laser pistol from the downstairs arsenal. Then he and Dr. Smith used one of the rear hatches and climbed out of the ship, leaving the hatch open so they could return unheard. They climbed cautiously down the steps of one of the landing legs. Before long they were standing on the surface of the planet.

Once on the ground he and Dr. Smith scurried around to the front of the ship and headed for the strange alien machine.

The rope ladder the alien had used to escape the machine was still dangling from its hatch. Will grabbed it and pulled himself up, constantly checking over his shoulder to make sure his mother couldn't see him from the viewport of the *Jupiter 2*. A few seconds later Dr. Smith followed.

"This doesn't look so bad from the inside," Will commented once he and Dr. Smith were inside the monster machine. "In fact, it just looks like a regular old space module. Look, Dr. Smith, it even has an old-fashioned nuclear-fusion engine and a positively ancient twelve hundred line resolution video monitor."

"Does that mean you'll be able to get this thing working again?" asked Dr. Smith.

Will began to fidget with some of the machine's controls.

Suddenly the control panel lit up and the hum of its computer drives began to kick in.

"It's booting up," said Will with surprise. "I must have just temporarily overloaded its system defenses when I shot it with the *Jupiter 2*'s laser."

A smile of relief crossed Dr. Smith's face. "Very good, my boy," he said. "Now, as soon as we close the hatch we can be on our way!"

As Dr. Smith turned to the still open hatch, he let out a scream. A dark, scaly hand had reached in from outside and grabbed him by the collar!

8
The Abandoned City

"Will, help me!" screamed Dr. Smith. "Whatever it is it's trying to choke me!"

Will quickly ran to Dr. Smith and tried to pull him away, but the attacking hand's grip was too great.

"I'm going to have to blast it!" said Will as he reached for his laser pistol.

"Hurry, Will! Hurry!" cried Dr. Smith.

Will pointed his pistol and aimed.

"Blawp, I told you to come back down!" a voice called from outside the hatch. It was Penny. And the hand that had grabbed Dr. Smith by the collar belonged to Blawp! It was using Dr. Smith to pull itself inside.

Suddenly Blawp released her grip on Dr. Smith as Penny appeared in the hatchway and took her in her arms.

Will quickly put down his gun. "Penny, what are you doing here?" he asked.

"I could ask you the same thing," replied his sister in an accusing tone of voice. "Somebody left the rear hatch of the *Jupiter 2* open and Blawp ran out. I guess I don't have to wonder who it was, huh? You know what Dad said about leaving the ship."

"You wouldn't understand," said Will.

"What a brainy thing to say, Will Robinson!" Penny snapped back. "Wait till I tell Mom what you're doing! You're not supposed to be in here at all!"

"Exactly what *I* was just about to tell your brother when I saw him sneaking out of the spaceship —" lied Dr. Smith, still out of breath from his encounter with Blawp.

"But, Dr. Smith, that's not true!" started Will. "This was all your idea!"

"Now, William," Smith interrupted. "Remember what we said about taking responsibility. You see, Penny, your brother courageously decided to try and restart this machine in the hopes that he could return it to the aliens in exchange for our freedom. A noble idea, wouldn't you agree?"

"I guess so . . ." said Penny, thinking about it.

"But, naturally, it's against the rules," finished Smith. "So when I came upon him here I was just about to return him to the ship. Of course, I wasn't going to tell your mother about any of this. It was just going to be our little secret."

"Well," Penny said thoughtfully. "I guess that was a good idea after all, Will. But just the same I think we ought to get back to the ship."

No sooner had she finished her sentence than Blawp jumped out of her arms and skipped deeper inside the machine's capsule. Fascinated by the flashing lights on the machine's control panel, Blawp began to press buttons wildly.

"Blawp, stop! Come back!" shouted Penny.

"Hey, stop her, Penny!" shouted Will. "She's playing around with the launch drive!"

But it was too late. Blawp had already flicked too many commands into the launch systems. There was a great rumbling beneath the machine as the thruster engines kicked in.

Will ran to the controls. "Blawp must have activated its launch sequence!" he observed.

They could feel the force of gravity push down on them as the alien machine lifted off.

"We're taking off!" exclaimed Penny. "Will, do something!"

"I'm trying," replied Will, who had already begun inputting countercommands into the controls. "But the controls won't respond! This ship's been preprogrammed!"

"I'd better access the machine's video systems," Penny told her brother. With a few simple entries into the machine's video console she managed to turn on its main monitors. On them everyone could see that the machine had lifted far off the ground and was now moving away from the *Jupiter 2*.

"Where are we going?" asked Dr. Smith.

"I don't know, Dr. Smith," replied Will. "Like I said, this machine has been preprogrammed. It's probably taking us back to where it came from. It looks like we'll just have to sit back and enjoy the ride."

"Look, Will," said Penny, pointing at the video monitor. "We're heading directly for the alien city."

"We're going in the same direction Dad and Major West went before they disappeared," said Will.

After traveling for nearly half an hour the alien machine reached the city. As it did so, it slowed down. Will and the others realized instantly that the machine's destination must be somewhere in the city.

They had a bird's-eye view, and watched with awe as images of the city appeared in the monitors. The city was enormous, larger than any they had ever seen back on Earth. The streets were crammed with buildings, many of them skyscrapers with towers that seemed to reach into the green clouds in the sky. The streets and avenues were connected by a complicated maze of monorails and bridges. These roads and railways were above the streets and occupied many different levels. Some areas seemed so dense with these structures that it was hard to see through them down to the streets.

Operating the spacecraft's video cameras, Penny skillfully zoomed in to get a closer look. It was impossible not to notice how unusually narrow everything was. The buildings, the walkways, the sidewalks, the entranceways: the people who lived in this city must be incredibly thin.

"Look, Will," said Penny. "There are trains running along those monorails. And they seem to be making regular stops."

"Everything seems to be working," Will observed. "The streetlights, those electric signs on some of those buildings. But who's operating them? I don't see any people."

"Look at that monorail station, Will," said Penny, zooming a camera in. "There's a crowd getting off that train."

It was a crowd, all right, Will agreed. But the passengers who got off the train were robots, just like the ones that had greeted the *Jupiter 2* when it first landed.

An eerie feeling came over Will. For although the city was busy with mechanical activity, they had yet to see one living soul.

"We're coming to a clearing," noticed Dr. Smith.

The machine had slowed down over a wide plaza that was situated inside a circle of buildings at the centermost part of the city.

"It's the chariot!" noticed Penny, zooming in with one of the cameras.

The *Jupiter 2*'s land rover was sitting right in the center of the plaza, but it was empty. Its doors were open, but neither the children's father nor Don West could be seen anywhere.

Suddenly the monster machine began to descend.

"We're landing," said Will. "Hold on!"

They braced themselves against the cramped walls as the primitive spacecraft slowly came down in the middle of the plaza. As soon as it landed its hatch popped open.

Nobody moved.

"Well," said Will after a minute. "I suppose we should go outside. I'll go first."

The rope ladder was still hanging off the side and Will used it as he carefully climbed through the hatch and lowered himself to the ground. In a few short minutes Penny, Blawp, and Dr. Smith had followed.

As soon as Penny's feet hit the ground, she gasped. "Look!" she exclaimed. "We're surrounded!"

Without warning the doors and rampways of the surrounding buildings had opened. Through them now emerged small troops of robots, the same strange collection of mechanical soldiers that had earlier surrounded the *Jupiter 2*.

They were coming from all directions and closing in fast.

9
Chased!

"They're headed straight for us!" exclaimed Dr. Smith. "Fire your pistol, Will! Fire!"

But Will wouldn't fire his laser. "Look, Dr. Smith," he said instead. "They're stopping just like before. I don't think they want to hurt us."

It was true. Just as they had after the *Jupiter 2* landed, the robots came to a full stop several feet away from Will and the others.

"We can't take any chances," said Dr. Smith. "Shoot them!"

"No way, Dr. Smith," insisted Will. "I want to find out what they want."

"If you won't shoot them then I will," said Dr. Smith. "Give me that!" He grabbed the laser pistol out of Will's hand. Then he aimed at one of the robots and fired. The robot exploded in a blaze of sparks and fell to the ground.

Then, all at once, the other robots began to rumble with movement. One of them raised an antenna and aimed it directly at Dr. Smith. There was a crisp clicking sound, then a laser bolt fired from an opening at the end of the antenna. The laser hit the gun in Dr. Smith's hand, vaporizing it instantly.

Next, all the robots began to swarm in on Will and the others like some angry mob.

"Now, you've done it, Dr. Smith!" said Will.

"They're going to kill us!" exclaimed Dr. Smith fearfully.

"Will, we'd better make a run for it!" shouted Penny.

"This way!" shouted Will.

Penny and Dr. Smith followed Will as he discovered some stairs that led them away from the plaza. Ahead of them was the city they had, up until now, only seen from above. Behind them the angry robots were closing in.

Will led the others around the corner of a nearby building. For the time being they were hidden from the robots' view.

"Well, what do we do now?" groaned Dr. Smith. "Just wait here until they come to get us?"

"They wouldn't be chasing us right now if you hadn't fired on them, Dr. Smith," said Will accusingly.

"Why do you say that, Will?" asked Penny before Dr. Smith could respond.

"Think about it, Penny," said Will. "Ever since we landed on this planet the robots have pretty much left us alone. Even when that alien was on board the ship it seemed more interested in the Robot than in us."

"You mean all they want is the Robot?" asked Penny.

"I think so," replied Will.

"But why? There are so many robots here. Why do they need one more?"

"If we knew that then maybe we could figure out some way to rescue *our* Robot, as well as Dad and Major West," said Will. "If only there were some way we could learn more about this planet."

Just then Blawp began to grunt with uncontrollable excitement. From out of nowhere, a rubber ball the size of a large melon had bounced down the street and come to a stop. Then, all on its own, the ball spun around and began to roll back from the direction it came.

Blawp leaped out of Penny's arms and chased the ball.

"Blawp, come back!" called Penny. She started down the street after the creature.

Will started to follow when Dr. Smith grabbed him by the arm.

"Will, wait," said Dr. Smith with a shudder. "We don't know what's down there!"

"But we sure know what's *back there*!" exclaimed Will, pointing behind Dr. Smith.

Dr. Smith swerved around and shrieked. The mob of robots had just appeared from around the corner and was slowly making its way toward them.

"Run for your life, Will!" Dr. Smith screamed. Then he swiftly darted away from the pursuing robots, nearly tripping over Will as he went.

Will and Dr. Smith ran as fast as they could. But after turning the same corner Penny had disappeared behind, they both came to an abrupt stop.

They were standing before a small concrete quadrant enclosed by a rickety wire gate. Inside the quadrant were several clusters of small robots no larger than an average human toddler. Some were climbing on a strange structure of metallic bars that reminded Will of monkey bars back on Earth. Others were simply flying playfully through the spaces between the bars. There was another structure with seats attached by long rods that lifted up and around, pushed only by the momentum of the small robots that were playing in it. *Swings?* Will wondered.

There were other structures as well, one reminding Will of a seesaw, another of a slide. Tiny, pint-sized robots were playing on all of them.

Nearby, some larger robots sat casually on benches, some alone, some together. One or two cylindrical headed ones were cradling tiny baby-sized robots in their arms. Suddenly two small box-shaped robots raced toward a wayward ball. When one refused to let the other play with it, a door opened on each of their heads and two jack-in-the-boxes sprung out. Before long they were swinging fists at each other. Upon seeing this a larger robot rushed over and popped out of its box-shaped hull. It quickly broke up the fight, all the while yelling at the tiny robots in a series of signals that Will could only interpret as a reprimand. It was just what parents might do back on Earth.

"Is this some kind of playground, Dr. Smith?" Will wondered aloud.

"Is it possible?" replied Smith, astonished. "Are these machines actually *civilized*?"

Will pointed at the monkey bars. "Look, there's Penny!" he said. Penny had chased Blawp to the top of the strange-looking monkey bars. She had just pulled her mischievous alien safely into her arms and was starting back down when she shouted to Will and Dr. Smith with alarm.

"Will! Dr. Smith! Look out!" she warned.

Will and Dr. Smith turned. The mob of robots that had been following them from the plaza was now entering the alien playground. Will hurried to help Penny down the last level of the monkey bars. Then the three of them started to run toward an exit on the other side.

Suddenly, without warning, came the high-pitched signal they had heard back when the alien kidnapped the Robot from the *Jupiter 2*. Once again they had to stop and cover their ears.

The sound seemed to come from out of nowhere. And it seemed to have an effect on all the robots in the playground. Large or small, the robots suddenly stopped whatever they were doing. The smaller robots climbed down off the monkey bars and swings and the larger ones rose up from the benches.

"They're being controlled by that signal!" Will pointed out. "Just like our Robot was when the alien kidnapped him!"

"I can't stand it!" yelled Dr. Smith. "That sound is making my head burst!"

"They're coming after us!" shouted Penny.

It was true. The robots of the playground had joined the robots from the plaza. Now the mob had nearly doubled in size.

"Let's get out of here!" shouted Will.

He and the others ran across the playground and out the other side. They found themselves running along a wide boulevard that was filled with flying cars, buses, and taxis, all operated by robots. Further along they came to a series of buildings and shops. Robots were coming in and out of them, many carrying shopping bags overflowing with items from the stores. One shop window displayed robots wearing the latest fashions. Another displayed the latest collection of magazines and newspapers all written in a strange alien language. Yet another showed a robot family taking a vacation in a sunny tropical paradise!

Then, just as in the playground, all the robots in the boulevard stopped what they were doing as soon as they heard the high-pitched siren. At once, they clustered together and poured into the street. They surged forward and blocked Will, Penny, and Dr. Smith from running any further. Will and the others tried to run away when they were suddenly confronted by the robots from the playground and the plaza.

"They're blocking our way!" Penny shouted as she tightened her arms around Blawp.

They were surrounded.

"Make way! Make way!" a mechanical voice came from the crowd.

At the sound of the command the robots suddenly moved aside.

"It's our Robot!" exclaimed Will with glee.

The *Jupiter 2*'s Robot was now making its way through the crowd.

Will sighed with relief at the sight of his mechanical friend. He ran up to it, his arms extended, ready to give it a big hug.

"Come no further, Will Robinson," the Robot ordered in an unusually cold tone of voice. He extended his arms, his laser claws cocked. "If you do I shall be forced to destroy you!"

10
The Hall of Science

"Put those arms down and explain yourself!" Dr. Smith snarled and walked up to the Robot.

"You are under arrest, Dr. Smith," replied the Robot.

"Arrest?" Dr. Smith asked in an insulted tone of voice. "By whose authority? I am your superior officer and that means you must obey *my* commands."

"You? My superior?" The Robot laughed, letting out a series of loud screeches. "I am smarter. I am stronger. I am bigger. You are not worthy of oiling my tractor gears."

Will was stunned by the strange change in the Robot's personality.

"Robot, what's happened to you?" he asked. "You don't sound like yourself."

"But I am myself, Will Robinson," replied the Robot. "Now march!"

The Robot prodded Will, Penny, and Dr. Smith ahead. In a short while they had returned to the clearing where the monster machine had landed. Nothing had changed. The monster machine, as well as the abandoned chariot, were still there in the center of the plaza.

The Robot led Will and the others into the largest building in the plaza. Its main door had been ripped open at the frame. Will could tell that the original frame of the door had once been very narrow, just like most of the other structures in the city. Will decided that someone must have ripped it open so that some of the robots on this planet could pass through unobstructed.

The Robot then led Will and the others through the building's lobby. As they walked Will noticed that there were some three-dimensional holographic images hovering along the walls. The holographs were of symbols, some of which Will recognized. There was the symbol for the subatomic atom, one of the smallest molecules Earth science had yet discovered. Next there was the symbol for DNA, the genetic basis for all life. There was even the symbol for nuclear fusion, which was the kind of power used during an early period of manned spaceflight.

Then there was a series of symbols that Will had never seen before.

"Penny, look at those symbols," Will pointed out to his sister. "Do you know what any of them mean?"

"Sure," replied Penny. "I recognize some of them."

"I think this building is some kind of Hall of Science," said Will. "Since we recognize some of those symbols it must mean that some science is universal. Take the one for the subatomic atom, for example. It could mean that all life is basically the same, but our atoms are just arranged differently."

"But there are a lot of signs I *can't* recognize," noted Penny.

"Maybe that's because we on Earth haven't discovered them yet," reasoned Will. "The civilization here could be much more advanced than our own."

"If that's so," wondered Penny, "how is it that the aliens' flying machine is more primitive than the *Jupiter 2*?"

"I don't know," said Will with a shrug. "Maybe they aren't as interested in space flight as humans are."

Next Will, Penny, and Dr. Smith were led into a turbolift by the Robot.

"Sublevel twenty-one-hundred-and-three," the Robot ordered the turbolift. A row of cylindrical bars enclosed the group within the mechanism and the turbolift dropped through the floor at an incredible speed.

It seemed as if they were falling for minutes. Yet, despite the speed of the drop, neither Will nor the others felt the slightest discomfort.

"Robot, where are you taking us?" asked Will.

"There is no need for you to know that, Will Robinson," replied the Robot in his new cold tone of voice.

"Are my father and Major West all right?"

"Those members of your party remain unharmed."

"Thank goodness for that," Penny said.

Will knew something was up with the Robot. But what?

"Robot, I promised I was gonna find out what went wrong with you and I'm still gonna do it," said Will.

"Wrong with me?" replied the Robot. "There is nothing wrong with me."

"Says you," groaned Dr. Smith.

"I am where I belong, Dr. Smith," insisted the Robot. "I am with my society."

"Robot, I know you're under somebody or some*thing's* power," continued Will. "I know you wouldn't do any of these bad things on your own."

"*Bad* things?" repeated the Robot. "That does not compute. I am only doing my duty."

Just then the turbolift came to a slow, soft stop.

"Follow me," said the Robot.

Will, Penny, and Dr. Smith followed the Robot off the turbolift. From the trip down Will realized that they must be thousands of feet below the surface of the planet. They were in a great cavernous room so high it had no ceiling and so deep it seemed to stretch forever into the darkness. After walking only a few short feet they came to an abrupt stop.

"How horrible!" Dr. Smith suddenly shrieked.

"Oh, no!" cried Penny. Even Blawp let out a horrified screech.

Will was simply speechless, his cry stuck in his throat. For just ahead of them was a large metallic sphere, about the size of a house. Extending from the sphere in all directions was a gooey web-like net. There were many things attached to the strange net, most of which looked like discarded versions of the robots Will and the others had seen outside. There were also some mangled skeletons that looked like they belonged to a variety of alien species. But that wasn't what had startled Will.

Pinned against the net, their arms and legs extended like helpless bugs, were his father and Major West.

11
The Eye of the Sphere

"Dad! Major West!" both Will and Penny exclaimed with alarm.

Professor Robinson and Major West did not reply. They were motionless. And although their eyes were wide open, they acted as if they didn't recognize Will and Penny at all.

"I thought you said they were unharmed!" Will said to the Robot.

"I assure you, Will Robinson," replied the Robot. "I knew nothing of this."

"Traitor!" Dr. Smith said to the Robot, accusingly. "You've killed them!"

"My sensors indicate that Professor Robinson and Major West are still alive," responded the Robot.

Just then the sphere began to whir and hum with mechanical life. Then two great lids opened in the center of it, revealing something that looked like a huge human eye.

"You have done well, Robot," a deep mechanical voice came from inside the sphere. The voice was so loud it echoed in the great depths of the room.

"By capturing these runaway peripherals you have com-

pleted your diagnostic mapping," the sphere told the Robot. *"Now you will be able to take your rightful place among the System."*

Just then Will moved a step forward. He would have walked right up to the giant sphere had Dr. Smith not held him back.

"Be careful, Will," warned Dr. Smith. "We don't know what kind of horrible power that thing has!"

But Will pulled away from Dr. Smith. "Why did you kidnap our Robot?" he asked the sphere. "And what have you done to my dad and Major West?"

"The human peripherals you speak of could not be downloaded," replied the sphere. *"Their neural impulses were neutralized during the process."*

"Neural impulses neutralized?" repeated Dr. Smith with a shiver. "You mean you've wiped their brains clean?"

Ignoring Dr. Smith, the sphere continued. *"As for the Robot, downloading has been successful. He is now of the System. The System can continue."*

"Will," whispered Dr. Smith. "The flying machine. Tell it about the flying machine."

"I know all about your plan," the sphere cut in. *"It would never have worked. Sooner or later the shuttlecraft you returned would have reactivated and returned to us on its own."*

Just then the Robot began to wave its arms. "Warning! Warning!" he shouted with alarm. "Hostiles approaching! Hostiles approaching!"

At the sound of the Robot's alarm an image appeared in the pupil of the sphere's eye. "It's Mom and Judy!" exclaimed Penny. They were flying toward the city wearing jet packs.

"Will! Penny!" Maureen and Judy could be heard calling from the sky. "Will! Penny! Where are you?"

"They've come looking for us," added Will. Then he shouted, "Mom! Judy! Get out of here! You're in danger!" Penny joined in, but it was soon clear that it was impossible for them to be heard.

"*How curious,*" said the sphere. "*Even though you send messages your human peripherals seem to act independently of any central programming core. No matter. Those two can be easily overwritten. GlimBus Two! GlimBus Two! Attend!*"

"Will," said Penny. "I think this thing is some kind of giant central computer brain. And it thinks we're part of another computer."

"That's my mother and my sister out there," Will told the sphere. "They're not computer parts. You can't just override them like you would a computer program."

"*Your language, like those of the two peripherals that came before you, is illogical,*" said the sphere. "*Your program must be flawed. No matter. Once reinitialized, you, like your Robot, will be downloaded. You will find your internal coprocessors will function much better once you have interfaced with the System. GlimBus Two! GlimBus Two! Where are you?*"

"I'm coming! I'm coming!" a voice was heard from the darkness beyond. "I heard you, System Prime. I heard you."

A small figure emerged from the darkness. Will and the others recognized it at once as the android boy who kidnapped the Robot from the *Jupiter 2.*

"*Your response time to my command was insufficient,*" the sphere scolded the android.

"I'm sorry," replied the android nervously in a voice that was as high and soft as its fragile appearance. "There were some very interesting new facts I was compiling in the science library —"

"*Facts? Facts?*" the sphere said angrily. "*You are constantly rearranging your menu's priorities, GlimBus Two! Must I rearrange your neural net?*"

"No, System Prime! No!" the android cried fearfully.

But it was too late. Once again the loud high-pitched siren was heard. The breastplate on the android's chest, the one that had seemed to control him back on the *Jupiter 2*, suddenly lit up with a pulsating light.

"Please, stop!" the android begged the sphere. "I won't be late again! I promise!"

In an instant his chestplate went dark.

"*Just a reminder, GlimBus Two,*" said the sphere. "*Next time you will be completely purged and reinitialized.*"

"What do you wish me to do, System Prime?" asked the android fearfully. "Tell me and I shall do it immediately!"

"*Since you did not destroy the humans as you were ordered to when I sent you to get their Robot, they are now invading our System. Like the first two, they must be stopped. Go and intercept the approaching hostiles immediately.*"

"Yes, System Prime," said the android as he scurried into the turbolift. "Immediately, sir! Immediately!"

Will, Penny, and Dr. Smith watched as Maureen and Judy landed feet first in the plaza outside and turned their jet packs off. As soon as they began to examine the empty chariot, a troop of robots, led by GlimBus Two, emerged and carried them away.

"Mom! Judy!" Will and Penny cried out.

"What are you going to do with them?" Dr. Smith asked the sphere.

"*They have been apprehended,*" replied the sphere. "*In a few moments they will be primed for downloading into the System.*"

"What do you mean?" asked Will.

"*All must be downloaded into the System,*" replied the sphere. "*The System must continue.*"

A cloud of orange gas shot out from the center of the sphere's eye. The fumes were so strong they made Will, Penny, and Dr. Smith cough.

"It's knockout gas!" shouted Will.

"*You will be temporarily immobilized,*" said the sphere. "*Then you, too, will be primed for downloading.*"

"But we're humans," said Penny. "You can't download us like you did the Robot. You can't just erase everything in our brains!"

"*All must be downloaded into the System,*" repeated the sphere. "*The System must continue. . . . The System must continue. . . . The System must continue. . . .*"

The giant sphere closed its great eye. It was the last thing Will and the others saw before passing out.

12
A Matter of Facts

When Will opened his eyes it took some time for his vision to clear. When it finally did, his heart skipped a beat at the face that hovered over him.

It was the strange android boy, the one the sphere called GlimBus Two.

Will made an effort to move away, but couldn't. He was strapped to a table.

"Stay away from me!" he shouted.

The android ignored Will and moved closer. Will braced himself for the worst, but to his surprise the android placed a finger across his lips.

"Shhh," he told Will. "You must be quiet or we'll be caught, that's a fact." Then he unbuckled the binding straps. Will was able to sit up.

Will was in some kind of laboratory surrounded by computers and equipment. Also in the room were three other tables. On them were Penny, Blawp, and Dr. Smith. They, too, were starting to wake up from the effects of the knockout gas. Will watched as the android freed them from their straps as well.

Dr. Smith nearly let out a scream at first sight of the alien. Will ran over and put his hand across Dr. Smith's mouth.

"Be quiet, Dr. Smith," said Will. "I think he's trying to help us."

"Yes, yes," said the android. "Help you, I am, that's a fact." He once again placed his finger over his lips so that the others would be quiet. Then he pointed to two figures that were standing near the door of the laboratory.

"Dad! Major West!" exclaimed Penny.

The two men were standing, eyes wide open, but with no expressions on their faces. On their chests were now the same kind of chestplates that the android wore.

"They're guarding you, that's a fact," said the android.

"What's wrong with them?" asked Penny. "Why don't they recognize us?"

"Reinitialized, they are," explained the android. "Internal drives purged. Random Access Memory stored in the System now. That's a fact. Come with me."

Will and the others followed the android as he led them to the door. As they were about to leave, Professor Robinson and Major West's chestplates lit up. Like two mindless zombies the men stepped in front of the door so that no one could get out.

That's when the android reached up and turned the knob on his own chestplate. Professor Robinson and Major West's chestplates immediately went dark. Now it was an easy matter to walk past them and out of the room.

"Let's go," said the android. Then he led Will and the others out of the laboratory.

They walked through dark empty space for some time.

"Where are we going?" asked Dr. Smith. "Where are you taking us?"

"Shh! Quiet!" said the android. "If we're caught our neural nets will be neutralized instantly and that's a fact!"

After a time they came to a stop. The android once again touched a knob on his chestplate. All of a sudden the space around them became bright with light, revealing that they were now standing in front of a giant-sized cone-shaped obelisk. The obelisk was at the center of a circle of shelves, shelves that extended as far and high as the eye could see.

"What is this?" Will asked.

"This is my assigned partition," replied the android.

"You mean this is where you work?"

"It is where I perform my programmed tasks, yes," answered the android.

"Computer disks," Penny said, taking a disk off a shelf. "Millions of them."

"Seven trillion, nine hundred billion, three hundred million, ten thousand, five hundred and three — and *counting*!" Glim-Bus Two said proudly.

"It's a library, Will," exclaimed Penny with astonishment. "An incredibly *immense* library!"

"Will?" the android repeated upon hearing Penny say Will's name. He took a disk off a nearby shelf and brought it to the cone-shaped obelisk. There were some strange markings on the obelisk. Under each marking was a slot. GlimBus Two inserted the disk into one of the slots.

"*My name is Will Robinson,*" Will's voice was heard coming from the obelisk. "*I'm from Earth. You're on the* Jupiter 2 *spaceship. We mean you no harm. I didn't mean to hurt you with our laser, but I thought you were going to take our Robot.*"

"That's a recording of what I said to you back on the *Jupiter 2*," said Will.

"Yes," said the android. "I have collected it as well as other data from your spaceship's computer banks."

"That would explain why you and that eye-thing know our language," said Penny.

"I know much, yes," said the android. "I know that you are Penny Robinson, Will's sister. And you are Dr. Zachary Smith. I know all of you," continued the android, "and I know all about you. You are from that planet called Earth — not a very factual name for your planet since it, like yourselves, is comprised mostly of water, not earth. I also know that you were on a mission to establish a new home on a planet called Alpha Prime with the goal of saving your species from extinction. And that because of Dr. Smith your ship veered off course and became lost in space."

Dr. Smith snapped back indignantly, "You have no right to make groundless accusations —!"

"No accusation, Dr. Smith. Fact!" said the android proudly. "I'm good at facts. In fact, I know many of them. I collect them, store them, file them, alphabetize them, prioritize them, and retrieve them. That's my job. Keeper of facts. Would you like to hear some? How about the entire history of the universe in terms of its factual content? It's really a very short list of mathematical equations that would only take a mere thousand years to list. Each one, of course, a fact."

"Some other time, maybe," said Will. "Right now I'm more concerned with rescuing my family, Major West, and the Robot. It might help if you told us who you are and why you're helping us."

"Oh, I *have* been remiss!" said the android apologetically. "It is important to retrieve facts in a logical order. Otherwise all facts would be a mixed-up mumble-jumble of nonsensical information. Of course, the first thing you *must* know is my name. I am called GlimBus Two and that's a fact. Not GlimBus One, or GlimBus Three, or even GlimBus Seven-thousand-and-thirty-three. Just GlimBus Two."

"Nice to meet you, GlimBus Two," said Will.

"Same here," said Penny.

"As for your second question," began GlimBus Two, "System Prime had sent me to get your Robot. Then I was also supposed to destroy you. But you helped me when I fell out of the shuttle —"

"You were wounded," said Penny. "At least we thought you were. We couldn't just leave you to die."

"Die?" asked GlimBus Two. "But you could have just reinitialized me and downloaded me into your own system."

"Look, like I told that big eye-thing back there," said Will, "we're not machines. We're human beings. We do things a little differently. We wouldn't leave you to die, even if you are an android. "

"Yes, yes," replied GlimBus Two. "Different you are, that's a fact. Fascinating. No network connecting your neural nets, no file sharing, no common interface. These are facts that defy my logic parameters."

"That's because we're not part of any computer," explained Will. "No one tells us what to do —"

"— except our parents," added Penny. "Although half the time they're usually wrong."

"But that's only because they're supposed to teach us what's right and wrong," explained Will. "In the end it's up to each of us to make our own choices. It's kind of like we're on our own."

"These are most different and interesting facts," said Glim-Bus Two with the enthusiasm of a scientist. "I have analyzed them. That is why I have learned that since you helped me, it is only logical that I help you. Behold . . ."

GlimBus Two took another disk from the table and slipped it into another slot on the obelisk. In response a ray beam shot out from the top of the obelisk and projected an image on the ceiling. It was a 3-D holographic readout of the *Jupiter 2*. The image was so large it reached from one corner of the ceiling to the other.

"My computer's sensors show that your spaceship is in full working order," he said, pointing to the holograph. "It would be an easy matter for us to return there and leave this planet."

"Leave?" said Will.

"Yes," replied GlimBus Two. "You see, I have learned so much about the universe from the computer libraries of other spaceships System Prime has captured —"

"You mean you've hijacked other spaceships?" interrupted Dr. Smith.

"Twelve million and one to date, including the *Jupiter 2*!" replied GlimBus Two. "There's always a peripheral that comes flying around in a nearby orbit. Then *zap!* System Prime pulls them into our gravitational field, downloads whatever he can, and enters them into the System. You know, this planet is getting fearfully overcrowded!"

GlimBus Two turned off the holograph image of the *Jupiter 2*.

"That's why I've decided I would like to visit other worlds," he said. "And the first world I would like to visit is your own Earth."

"Earth?" asked Dr. Smith, eagerly. "Are you telling me you know the way back to Earth? Back home?"

"Do I know the way?" replied GlimBus Two. "Why Dr. Smith, once in space I could return you to Earth in less than one light-year — megahertz, of course!"

13
The Library

"Sorry, GlimBus Two," said Will. "But we're not leaving this planet without the others and the Robot."

"I do not understand," said GlimBus Two. "Those peripherals you speak of are now part of the System. They're not going anywhere."

"They're our family and friends," said Penny. "And we love them. If we can't leave with them, it isn't worth leaving at all."

"Now wait a moment, children," said Dr. Smith. "Have you forgotten your command training? As the only survivors it is our duty to make it back to the ship and escape. And if this charming android here is willing to show us the way back home, shouldn't we go with him? Later, after we return to Earth, we can send a rescue ship back here for the others."

"We're not the only survivors, Dr. Smith," said Will. "Dad and Don are still alive. And we don't know what happened to Mom and Judy."

"You mean you won't take me away from here?" asked GlimBus Two, lowering his head glumly. "Then I'll never get to have a mind of my own!"

"Why do you say that?" asked Penny. "I thought you were happy collecting facts in this library."

"How can anybody be happy doing something when they don't even know why they're doing it?" asked GlimBus Two. "Didn't you see what it's like outside? Around here nobody has a mind of their own. We only do what System Prime programs us to do. It's always 'GlimBus Two do this or GlimBus Two do that.' Why, you yourselves saw how he treated me. He treats everybody that way. Everyone around here goes along day in and day out doing things without the foggiest idea why they do them! They work in the stores, they ride the trains, they play in the playground. Always the same ones doing the same things. You never see anyone from the playground take the train. And you never see anyone from the train work in a store!"

"Why don't you just reprogram the System?" asked Will.

"Reprogram the System?" GlimBus Two laughed. "Reprogram the System? Unthinkable! Laughable! Impossible! Only System Prime can reprogram anything around here and I assure you he's happy with things just the way they are!"

"Why, that ugly old eye is just an overstuffed computer drive," said Penny. "Someone had to create his program. What happened to the people who used to live on this planet?"

"The people? What people?"

"The people who must have built the city," said Will. "It's obviously not designed for the robots."

GlimBus Two paused. "System Prime designed by the people?" he asked, thoughtfully. "Mmmm. Do you know this for a fact?"

"It's just an educated hunch," replied Will.

"A — *hunch?*" asked GlimBus Two, perplexed. "According to my analysis of your language a hunch is defined as a lump, a hump, or a chunk. I see no such structure on your body."

"It's just a feeling we humans get when we know something is right," explained Penny.

"It doesn't sound like a very good foundation to base a fact on," said GlimBus Two.

"Look, I can't make any promises, GlimBus Two," said Will. "But there may be a way for us to help each other. It may not be a fact, but it's all I can offer."

GlimBus Two thought for a moment. "I believe I am getting a hunch, as well," he said. "Tell me how I can help you."

"I think you have more answers than you know," Will told the friendly android. "And they're right here." Will pointed to the giant obelisk in the center of the room.

"I don't understand," replied GlimBus Two.

"It's my guess that the entire history of this planet is somewhere in this computer library," explained Will. "I don't care how long it takes, but if we start now we may be able to find a way to reprogram the System! GlimBus Two, if I gave you the category, could you find the right disk?"

"I suppose I could run a cross-reference program and come up with some possibilities."

"William," said Dr. Smith. "Are you aware how long it would take us to put together the correct programs to overthrow that asteroid-sized brain — even if we could narrow it down to a few thousand disks?"

"I believe it could take anywhere from three-point-five hours to six-point-seven-years, Dr. Smith," computed Glim-Bus Two.

"Robots," groaned Dr. Smith. "They're all alike!"

Will, Penny, and GlimBus Two ignored Dr. Smith's comment and began to make their way through the computer disks in the library. Dr. Smith checked off each disk when they were done reading it. And Blawp helped out by using its long monkey-like arms to climb to the topmost shelves and retrieve disks.

With each inserted disk the obelisk displayed an immense holographic readout on the ceiling of the room. Some disks showed geological information of the planet, such as its plant and mineral life. Some showed the position of the planet in its solar system. Some even showed records of other parts of the universe, just as GlimBus Two had described.

They had hardly worked for half an hour when, without warning, the sound of the high-pitched alarm filled the room.

"*GlimBus Two!*" the voice of System Prime came over the obelisk. "*This time you have gone too far!*"

"It's System Prime!" panicked GlimBus Two. "I knew it was only a matter of time before he found out what we were doing. We should have escaped while we had the chance. Now we're done for! Run! Run!"

And with that GlimBus Two began to run in all directions.

"Hey, where's Dr. Smith?" asked Penny, grabbing little Blawp in her arms.

"I thought he was cataloging disks," said Will.

But Will was wrong. There was a pile of disks at a table where Dr. Smith had been working. They were all untouched. And Dr. Smith was nowhere to be found.

"Dr. Smith!" called Will and Penny as they searched the library. "Dr. Smith, where are you?"

Before they could search thoroughly, they found themselves face-to-face with their Robot. He was flanked by Professor and Mrs. Robinson, Major West, and Judy, all of whom were now wearing a pulsating chestplate on their suits.

"Arrest them!" the Robot commanded the adults.

The four adults seemed to have no minds of their own. Obeying without question they moved with zombie-like stiffness toward the children.

14
Recaptured!

Within minutes Will, Penny, and GlimBus Two were brought before System Prime. Its eye stared down at them angrily.

"*GlimBus Two, you have acted independently of the System,*" accused System Prime. "*Explain yourself.*"

"I can't help myself, System Prime," replied GlimBus Two, his head lowered. "Perhaps it would be better if you completely purged my programming!"

"No, wait!" said Will, stepping forward. "You can't just wipe out GlimBus Two's programming!"

"*Silence!*" System Prime shouted at Will. A bright ray shot out of the sphere's eye that paralyzed GlimBus Two where he stood. Then the sphere turned its eye back to Will and Penny.

"*In a few minutes you, like your companions, will be downloaded,*" said System Prime. "*Then the System will once again continue uninterrupted.*"

"Unhand me!" a familiar voice was suddenly heard.

"It's Dr. Smith!" said Penny.

At that very moment Dr. Smith was being led before the sphere by the Robot.

"Dr. Smith, are you all right?" asked Will.

"I will be once this monstrous machine releases me," said Dr. Smith as he yanked himself from the Robot's grasp.

"What happened to you?" asked Will.

"I was going about my business cataloging disks in the library when all of a sudden our old friend the Robot abducted me and forced me to tell them of your plans!"

"That is a lie, Dr. Smith," said the Robot.

"A lie, indeed!" said Dr. Smith. "Everybody knows your intentions are no longer friendly!"

"You sneaked away from the library and offered information of the children's plans to System Prime in exchange for safe passage back to Earth," said the Robot.

"Dr. Smith, what a *pal* —!" said Penny sarcastically.

"I assure you, Penny," said Dr. Smith, obviously changing his story. "I had only your best interests at heart. I explained to System Prime that if it's robots he's looking for, then Earth is the place to shop! I simply offered to act as a negotiator between our two worlds — in exchange for all of our safety. And now, as you'll see, I have been brought here to put the final touches on our agreement."

Dr. Smith walked up to the great eye of System Prime.

"What do you say, System Prime?" Dr. Smith asked the sphere with an eager smile. "The children's plan has been stopped. Do we have a deal?"

System Prime let out a boisterous mechanical laugh.

"*I do not make deals with peripherals,*" it replied. "*Reinitialize him!*"

Upon that order the Robot, together with the zombie-like Professor Robinson and Major West, grabbed Dr. Smith.

"What?" cried Dr. Smith. "Where are you taking me?"

They carried Dr. Smith to a small nearby chamber.

"You can't do this to me!" shouted Dr. Smith. "We had a deal!"

But the sphere ignored Dr. Smith's cries. The Robot and the others placed Dr. Smith inside the chamber. The chamber began to hum and pulsate. The sounds became so loud that they soon drowned out Dr. Smith's screams.

Suddenly a hatch opened from System Prime's round hull. A cable shot out and clasped itself onto Dr. Smith's chest. It remained there for a long moment.

Will watched in horror as all the color drained from Dr. Smith's face. Soon Dr. Smith's eyes, once wide open with fear, held no expression at all.

Finally, the cable retracted, leaving behind a chestplate on Dr. Smith, the same kind that was worn by GlimBus Two and the others. Next, the humming and pulsating of the chamber died down. Dr. Smith stood perfectly silent and at attention.

"*Come to me!*" System Prime ordered Dr. Smith.

Dr. Smith's chestplate lit up. He marched out of the chamber and walked up to the great eye. Now he, too, was a zombie.

"*You are now of the System,*" System Prime told Dr. Smith. "*The System must continue.*"

"I am of the System," repeated Dr. Smith without emotion. "The System must continue."

"They've wiped Dr. Smith's brain clean!" exclaimed Penny with horror. "And they're going to do the same to us!"

15
No Way Out

"*It is time*," said the voice in the sphere. "*Robot, bring the one called Will Robinson to the reinitializing chamber.*"

The Robot obediently moved to Will.

"No!" Penny cried out, grasping Blawp tighter in her arms. "You can't! You can't!"

"*Silence her!*" commanded the sphere. Will watched helplessly as Mrs. Robinson and Judy mindlessly brought Penny closer to the sphere. Once again the sphere shot its bright paralyzing ray from the pupil of its eye. The ray first surrounded Penny, then froze her into silence.

"You must come with me, Will Robinson," said the Robot reaching out for Will's arm.

Will knew now that there was no way out of this terrible situation. His parents, Judy, Major West, and Dr. Smith were now under the complete control of System Prime: unable to be absorbed by the massive computer, their thoughts were completely erased. The Robot was now a servant of the System: reprogrammed to take its place among the millions of robots that lived on this planet. And GlimBus Two, perhaps his only hope for escape, would probably soon be reinitialized and re-programmed as well.

"It's all right, Robot," Will said, bravely pulling his arm away from the Robot. "I know the way."

Will took a few steps toward the chamber.

"Wait a minute," he said. Then he stopped and turned to face the great eye of System Prime.

"You may have beat us this time," said Will. "But pretty soon someone will figure out a way to stop you. You can't control everything forever. Everything deserves a chance to be free, to decide things on their own, to think their own thoughts. You're just a machine. I don't know where you came from, or who built you, or *why*, but somebody someday is gonna figure out a way to pull your plug. And I hope I'll be here to see it!"

Will followed the Robot and stepped into the reinitializing chamber. The chamber lit up, imprisoning Will inside.

"Well, I guess this is good-bye, Robot," Will said.

"Yes, Will Robinson," said the Robot. "This is good-bye."

"I hope you're going to be happy here, Robot."

"I have taken my rightful place in the System," replied the Robot. "I am the new Chief of Police. I will have the respect of the other robots here."

"I have respect for you, Robot," Will said sincerely. "And so does the rest of my family. And even Dr. Smith, in his own way, well, I know he kind of likes you."

"My memory chips have pleasing sub-files of all of you as well," replied the Robot.

Will was surprised. He wondered how the Robot could still access his memory sub-files if he had been reinitialized by System Prime.

"Robot, I want you to know that no matter what happens, I don't blame you."

"Blame, Will Robinson?" asked the Robot.

"Yeah, you know," said Will. "Like when my mom caught us stealing the ice cream when we were up in space? I guess sometimes some things are out of your control. What I'm saying is, I forgive you for hijacking the ship and chasing us down and everything."

"Forgive —?" said the Robot. "You forgive me, Will Robinson?"

"Yes, Robot. Don't forget, we're still friends. Friends forgive each other."

"Friends?" asked the Robot.

"Sure," said Will. "We're practically brothers."

"Brothers," repeated the Robot. "The word seems familiar to me."

"*Step aside, Robot,*" came the voice of System Prime. "*Reinitialization must begin now.*"

Suddenly the Robot began to hum with internal electronic activity. Instead of moving away from the reinitializing chamber he remained close to Will.

"What's wrong, Robot?" asked Will.

"I like rainbow-colored sprinkles," replied the Robot.

Will smiled. It was one of his own likes as well, one that he had once programmed into the Robot. It was one of the things that made the Robot such a good friend.

"Me, too, Robot," said Will, sadly realizing he and the Robot might never share ice cream again.

"*We are like two mischievous brothers.*"

Will smiled again. The Robot was now remembering what Will's mom called them when she caught them sneaking the ice cream.

"That's right, Robot," he said. "We are."

"We are friends," said the Robot.

"Yeah," agreed Will. "We'll always be friends."

Now it suddenly hit Will what was happening. Something Will said must have stimulated the Robot's neural net. Somehow, Will realized, his own personality engrams, the ones he once implanted in the Robot, had survived. If that was so, if the Robot still had one fraction of a computer chip of loyalty left, then perhaps there was still a chance to get its help.

"Robot," Will began cautiously. "What do friends do?"

The Robot paused as it accessed its memory banks. "Friends forgive each other," replied the Robot.

"Exactly," said Will. Now he probed deeper, "And they protect each other."

"Protect each other . . ."

"Yeah. They help each other out of a jam."

"A jam?"

The Robot was faltering, obviously confused by Will's words.

"You are taking too long, Robot," System Prime said angrily. *"Step out of the way."*

Now the Robot's internal machinery was going wild. "I am experiencing a systems conflict," said the Robot. "I must run a diagnostic on my programming."

"Hurry, Robot!" said Will, crossing his fingers for luck. "Hurry!"

By the electronic sounds the Robot was making Will could tell it already had begun to analyze itself.

"You are conducting activity outside of the System," System Prime accused the Robot. *"This is not permitted."*

"I am discovering a mutation in my programming," replied

the Robot. "There are several corrupted files in my internal drive."

"That's it, Robot!" said Will excitedly. "Those corrupted files! That's the virus that's controlling you! Try running a bypass update on your Master Directory Block!"

"Computing!" replied the Robot. "I have isolated the corrupted files. I can now wipe them clean and modify my original templates."

"*Stop!*" System Prime ordered the Robot. "*I command you!*"

But the Robot did not stop. Will knew it couldn't if it wanted to. It had already begun to purge System Prime from its drive.

"*You will be destroyed!*" said System Prime. "*You will be neutralized!*"

At System Prime's command a troop of mechanical soldiers descended upon the Robot. They pulled the Robot away from Will.

"*The boy will be mine!*" shouted System Prime.

The hatch on the sphere's side opened and the long reinitializing cable shot out. It was headed straight for Will.

"Danger, Will Robinson!" said the Robot. "Danger!"

Will beamed upon hearing the Robot say those words. His Robot was back!

The Robot extended its arms. One by one it shot each of the attacking robots with a laser bolt, blowing them to bits. Then it sped between Will and the oncoming monster-sized cable.

"Robot, no!" cried Will.

But it was too late. The cable had attached itself to the Robot's hull.

16
Escape!

Almost instantly upon contact with the monster-sized cable, the Robot began to glow with electric light. Will knew that power from the cable, power that was meant for him, was now surging through the Robot. He doubted the Robot could survive.

The cable lifted the Robot and shook it high above ground. Then, after a few tense moments, the electricity went dead. The Robot became detached from the cable and fell helplessly to the ground.

"Robot!" shouted Will. He wanted to run to his friend, but could not pass through the invisible force field that kept him trapped in the reinitialization chamber. "Robot, are you okay?"

"I am weak, Will Robinson," said the Robot. "But I am unharmed. However, I am afraid my attempt to break free of System Prime was not successful. I still feel a connection to the System."

Suddenly a loud laugh came from the sphere. It was System Prime.

"*Did you think you puny peripherals could be any match*

for the System?" System Prime gloated. *"The System will con-tinue!"*

But Will ignored System Prime. He was more concerned with the Robot.

"It's all right, Robot," he told his friend gently. "You did your best."

"Will Robinson," said the Robot. "Do you still forgive me?"

"You're my best friend, Robot," Will said without hesitation. "Of course I forgive you."

"Forgive?" System Prime suddenly interjected. *"What is 'forgive'?"*

Will was momentarily startled by the question. It was very uncharacteristic of System Prime.

"Forgiveness is when one person excuses another for doing something wrong," Will told the giant sphere.

At that the sphere went into a tizzy of electronic noise.

"Forgiveness does not compute," said the sphere. *"What is happening to me? There is an error in my programming. I have a sudden urge for rainbow-colored sprinkles."*

Will didn't know exactly what had happened, but something had changed the sphere. It was now repeating things the Robot had said to Will in the past.

"Robot, can you hear me?" asked Will.

"Yes, Will Robinson," the Robot replied from the floor.

"Something's happened to System Prime. Can you ana-lyze?"

"Affirmative," replied the Robot. "My sensors show that System Prime's command protocols have been overridden by my neural net. It must have happened when I intercepted the reinitialization cable."

That could only mean one thing, Will knew. System Prime was now on-line with the Robot, rather than the other way around. It also meant that System Prime — and probably all the rest of the robots on the planet — were now infused with Will's own personality!

"What is happening to me?" asked System Prime. *"I do not understand. Will Robinson, do you forgive me?"*

"Sure." Will shrugged. "I forgive you."

"No! No! No!" said the sphere, sounding very confused. *"I do not need your forgiveness. I am System Prime! The System must continue! The System must continue! Forgive . . . Attack . . . Forgive . . . Attack . . . !"*

At that all the robots that stood guard around the sphere began to move about in all directions. Without warning they began to attack — each other!

"Robot, what's happening?" asked Will.

"System Prime is experiencing programming conflicts within itself," explained the Robot. "My sensors indicate that all the robots on the planet are now fighting one another. It is a fight that can only end in the destruction of every machine on this planet!"

"Forgive! Attack!" continued System Prime. *"Forgive! Attack!"*

The force field that had paralyzed GlimBus Two and Penny now suddenly released them. They ran to the reinitialization chamber where GlimBus Two was able to free Will.

"Are you two all right?" asked Will.

"Yes, yes, I'm fine," replied GlimBus Two. "And that's a fact."

"Me, too," said Penny.

Blawp screeched that she was all right, too.

"Hurry," said GlimBus Two. "We must escape before System Prime comes back to his senses."

"Wait!" said Will. "The Robot!"

Together the three managed to get the Robot to its feet.

"Can you move, Robot?" asked Will.

"My joint casings are a little out of balance," replied the Robot. "But I am mobile."

"Hurry!" said GlimBus Two. "We must escape!"

"We can't leave without the others!" said Will.

"Leave that to me," replied GlimBus Two. He turned a knob on his chestplate and aimed it at Professor and Mrs. Robinson, Major West, Judy, and Dr. Smith. In response to GlimBus Two's signal they obediently stood at attention.

"They will now go where I command them to go," said Glim-Bus Two.

"We've got to get back to the *Jupiter 2* and get off this planet," said Will.

"Negative, Will Robinson," warned the Robot. "The planet's surface is no longer safe for escape. We would not survive the journey."

"Then we've got to get back to the library," said Will. "With the Robot with us maybe we can find a way to repair System Prime and stop the fighting."

"It's worth a try," said Penny.

GlimBus Two set his beam on the Robinsons, Major West, and Dr. Smith. Then he led them and the others back to the library. But even the library was filled with battling robots. The fighting was so intense that many of the shelves had fallen and many of the computer disks had been ruined.

"Oh, my! Oh, no!" exclaimed GlimBus Two as he and the others arrived. "The facts! The facts! They're destroying all the facts! I must save them!"

GlimBus Two began picking up as many disks as he could from the floor.

"My sensors indicate that nearly ninety-seven percent of

the information stored in these disks has been destroyed, Will Robinson," said the Robot. "Our only option now is to hide somewhere until the robots destroy each other completely."

"But where can we hide, Robot?" asked Will.

"My sensors show a possible hiding place located in the center of this room," replied the Robot.

Will looked around. The only thing in the center of the room was the giant obelisk, the computer that projected its information on the ceiling.

"You mean that computer?" asked Will. "It's too small to hide all of us."

"It is not just a computer, Will Robinson," replied the Robot. "It is a doorway leading to an underground cavern of immense proportions."

"But how does it open?" asked Penny as she looked up and down the obelisk. "I don't see any way to open it."

"I have an immediate understanding of its technology due to my link-up with System Prime," said the Robot. "Like so much of the machinery on this world it can be controlled by a sub-frequency."

"Can you send the right signal to open it?" asked Will.

"I will try," replied the Robot.

The Robot began emitting a series of high-pitched signals. He tried one after another, but none of them worked.

"There is one more frequency left," said the Robot. "I will try it."

Again the Robot let out a high-pitched frequency. Again the obelisk did not budge an inch.

"I guess you were mistaken about the obelisk being a door, Robot," said Will.

"That does not compute, Will Robinson," said the Robot.

"Look," said Penny, pointing to GlimBus Two. "The signal's working."

Will and the Robot turned to look at the android. At the sound of the last signal his chestplate had popped open. Inside, was a small compartment with a computer diskette.

"What is it?" asked GlimBus Two, seeming as surprised as the others to find something inside his chestplate.

"That," said the Robot, "is the key to the obelisk's door!"

17
The Obelisk

Will removed the diskette from GlimBus Two's chestplate and studied it. It was unlabelled.

"Well, I'll be," said GlimBus Two. "I had no idea! Was that thing on me all this time? Where did it come from? Who put it there?"

"You mean you don't know?" asked Penny.

GlimBus Two shook his head.

"I bet it was put there by someone who wanted you to use it," said Will.

"But who could that be?" asked Penny.

"There's only one way to find out," said Will. He slipped the diskette into one of the drive slots on the obelisk.

The obelisk booted up instantly, just as it had when Will and the others were searching the computer library for the secret of System Prime. Then it stirred. Everyone heard a loud click. The obelisk gently pulled apart, leaving a narrow slit down its middle.

"It's an opening," said Penny.

"I guess we better see what's inside," said Will. He stepped close to the obelisk and tried to pry the opening further apart.

The obelisk was made of a heavy, thick metal and Will could barely nudge it. GlimBus Two and Penny each grabbed a piece of the opening and tried to help. Still, the heavy obelisk barely budged.

"Allow me," said the Robot. Then it stepped between the children and pried the obelisk apart as if it were a cracked eggshell.

Inside were the inner workings of a complex computer system. Thousand of tiny circuits, motherboards, and batteries shimmered with activity. The circuitry remained intact, connected by special wires that seemed designed to keep the computer running even after someone had pulled the obelisk apart.

The circuitry gave way at the bottom. There a flight of metallic stairs, each one lit by a row of tiny light reflectors, led down into a deep, dark emptiness.

"The Robot was right," said Penny. "There is something down there."

"The fighting here is getting worse," said the Robot. "I suggest we descend the stairs."

Everyone agreed. Following Will's lead, Penny, Blawp, and the Robot made their way into the obelisk. With his hand guiding them by the knobs on his chestplate, GlimBus Two directed Will's parents, Major West, Judy, and Dr. Smith into the obelisk as well.

There were many stairs and it seemed to take a long time to descend them. Most of their descent the space was dark, but after a while they saw a light at the bottom. As they climbed further down the light grew brighter. Soon the light began to take shape. By the time everyone reached the bottom of the stairs they could clearly see the shapes in the light.

They were the shapes of people. Thousands of them, perhaps tens of thousands. They were all suspended in the air at different levels by some unseen force. They lay flat, arms and legs extended, each one engulfed in a bright glow of light. Although they were of many different colors and sizes they all had one thing in common: they looked almost exactly like GlimBus Two.

"Are they dead, Robot?" asked Will.

"Negative, Will Robinson," said the Robot. "They are merely in a state of suspended animation, kept alive by that light that surrounds them."

"You mean, they're sleeping?"

"Yes," replied the Robot. "And by my calculations they have been that way for many centuries."

"They look just like you, GlimBus Two," said Penny.

GlimBus Two looked dumbstruck as he walked around the strange sleeping bodies. "I do not understand," he said. "This is a most interesting fact. Most interesting, indeed!"

"Maybe they're androids, too," said Penny.

"Negative, Penny Robinson," said the Robot. "These are biological life-forms, as alive as you or your brother."

Just then a hand of one of the sleeping beings stirred. Then its arm dropped, accidentally striking GlimBus Two in the back of the head.

"It's attacking me!" GlimBus Two cried, startled.

"Negative, GlimBus Two," said the Robot. "I believe it is simply waking up. It is possible by our opening the obelisk door we have deactivated their hibernation stasis."

The Robot was right. One by one the strange alien beings began to stir. Still floating in mid-air they stretched and yawned and rose as if from a long, restful nap. Eventually the glow that surrounded them dimmed, but not completely. What light was left seemed to lower the beings until they were standing on the ground.

One by one the beings approached and then surrounded Will and the others. Will noticed how thin and frail they were. It occurred to him that these must be the people who had designed the city above. They didn't frighten Will and he could see that Penny and Blawp were not frightened either. The beings seemed peaceful and gentle as they approached. And when they spoke, which they all did at once, it was in a soft tone of voice, almost a whisper. And it was in a language he could not understand.

"What are they saying, Robot?" asked Will.

But it was GlimBus Two who answered, "I understand what they are saying, Will Robinson," he said. "They are speaking a language that, for some reason, I seem to know."

"That is understandable, GlimBus Two," came a voice from the crowd. The voice spoke in English and belonged to one of the beings. The being seemed older than many of the others, but no less gentle. "After all," the being finished, "you were created by us. By *me*, to be more precise."

"Who are you?" asked GlimBus Two.

"My name is the same as yours," said the being. "It is the name I gave you when I created you. You might even call me GlimBus the First."

GlimBus Two studied his creator, eyeing him up and down. "You created me?" he asked, astonished. "Pardon me, but is that a *fact?*"

"An indisputable one," replied GlimBus the First, with a chuckle.

"Excuse me, sir," said Will. "I'm Will Robinson from the planet Earth —"

"Yes, I know," said the older GlimBus, interrupting him. "I know all about each and every one of you. I also know about the condition your poor family and friends are in. This will be quickly rectified, I assure you."

"How do you know these things?" asked Penny.

"The same way I know your language after only hearing a few words of it," replied GlimBus the First. "Yes, Will, your observation was correct when you were brought through our Hall of Science. Our studies did not focus on intergalactic space travel. We spent our history studying the powers of the mind."

"Hey, you're reading my thoughts!" exclaimed Will. "That's how you know our language!"

"Yes," said GlimBus the First. "Our knowledge and intelligence are billions of years beyond those of your species. We are capable of mental telepathy, communicating with other living beings by the power of our minds. Fascinating, Will. What is in your thoughts is almost unbelievable. It is hard to believe that our entire planet is now controlled by robots."

"You mean, you didn't know?" asked Penny.

"I only know what I am now learning from your thoughts, Penny," said GlimBus the First. "I can tell from your thoughts that some of these robots are evil. But how is that possible? GlimBus Two, did something go wrong with your programming?"

"I am programmed to collect the facts," replied GlimBus Two. "I have never shirked from my duty. Well, almost never."

"Yes, maintaining and updating the library was one of your directives," said GlimBus the First. "We knew there would be much information for us to catch up on when we awoke. But when we left you in charge it was simply to make sure the city remained in operation until our return."

"Me?" asked GlimBus Two. "In *charge?* Is that, too, a fact?"

"I get the feeling something has gone wrong," said GlimBus the First. "Terribly wrong. Only I'm not sure what. Perhaps your Robot can help me. By your calculations, Robot, based upon the biological evidence of my body, how long have we been in suspended animation?"

"According to my sensors you have been asleep for nearly five thousand years," replied the Robot.

GlimBus the First was speechless. There was a murmur of shock from the other recently awoken beings.

"That explains quite a bit," said GlimBus the First.

"What do you mean, sir?" asked Penny.

"It appears my people and I have overslept," replied the elder alien. "You see, we had set our alarm clock for only *five* years!"

18
Return of the Dolians

"My sensors indicate that the fighting is over," said the Robot. "It is now safe to return to the city."

It was only a few hours later when the noise from the clashing robots above had stopped. Everyone climbed the long dark staircase that led back to the computer library, each person dreading what they might find.

Will was the first to reach the top of the stairs and walk back through the opening in the obelisk. Around him the library lay in complete ruin. Robots lay on the floor, destroyed. Fires had been started and now almost every computer disk was melted beyond use. The obelisk, which once hummed as the central computer intelligence of the library, was now a dead mass of fused and burnt circuitry.

"That's the end of it," cried GlimBus Two, upon seeing the condition of the room. "It's hopeless. All my facts gone forever."

The aliens, led by the original GlimBus, were also saddened by the sight. Although they all had learned what had happened to Will and his family during the past few hours, they could only guess how their planet became a world of robots.

"We Dolians were a scientific race," GlimBus the First had told them while they waited down below for the fighting to end. "We spent centuries absorbed in our studies, which were mostly those of biology and geology. We felt the most important thing was to understand nature. By doing that we had hoped to cure any disease possible, thereby making certain that our species would exist forever. In later years we turned to genetics. Before long we were pure and healthy. Our people began to live longer and longer. I myself am several centuries old."

"Wow," said Will. "You mean you can live forever?"

"Nothing can live forever, as we soon learned," answered GlimBus the First. "You see, we had no interest in venturing into outer space because we did not want to be contaminated with any alien diseases. We forgot to consider the desire of other species to explore the stars. Eventually, one such alien crash-landed in a spaceship in one of our tropical jungles. It brought with it new diseases we had no defenses for. The alien quickly died. Soon after, the disease it brought here sent a plague around our world. Millions of our people became sick and perished."

"That was probably a virus of some kind," interjected Penny.

"Exactly," said GlimBus. "Our research told us that the disease — or *virus*, as you call it — would eventually die out. Only we would all be dead long before it did. We decided to flee below the surface and hibernate in this germ free chamber for five years. This was the period of time we determined it would take the disease to disappear. We quickly created a central computer program that would operate our cities and keep them from falling into ruin while we slept."

"That big eye-thing was your invention?" asked Penny.

"Yes. But we still needed something or someone to make sure the computer didn't malfunction. That's when I created an android. I named him GlimBus Two, after myself. I even implanted my own brain engrams on his circuitry so that he would behave like a true Dolian. It was GlimBus Two's job to maintain the computers, monitor the city, warn other passing aliens of the dangers of the disease and collect and organize all new scientific data for us to learn when we woke up."

"I always made sure to collect the facts," said GlimBus Two proudly. "And there were so many facts to collect."

"And a fine job you did, too," the original GlimBus replied. "However, after five years you were to hear a pre-programmed signal in your chestplate. Upon this signal your programming would have told you to awaken us. We would then have resumed our rightful place on our planet."

"But something went wrong," said Will. "Somehow the computer took over your planet."

"Apparently so," replied GlimBus the First. "The result of some internal system conflict or computer virus, we may never know. If what I read in your thoughts is true, the main computer became an all-powerful dictator, occasionally summoning robots from passing starships and downloading them into its database. In many ways it thought it was doing the right thing: It created a society of robots that kept the city running. Only it forgot to awaken us, the true inhabitants of the city."

"Its faulty computer program made GlimBus Two its servant, instead of its master," said the Robot. "And all computers must have a master."

Now, as they wandered through the ruins of what was once a thriving computer complex, GlimBus the First became disenchanted. The sphere that had come to call itself System

Prime was now completely dead. It had even broken apart, its internal circuitry sprawled haphazardly from its shell.

"The damage is great," said GlimBus the First. "Without the computer's database I may never be able to restore your parents and the others to their normal state. That is where all of their memories were stored."

Will's heart sank. And Penny began to sob.

19
Seventy-Two-Point-Nine Percent or Nothing . . .

"Wait a minute," said Will. "I have an idea! The database from System Prime! Robot, you said before that you were still connected to the System."

"That is correct, Will Robinson," replied the Robot. "Much of System Prime's logic board is still stored in my drive, although its command protocol has been terminated."

"Can you restart it?" ·

"To do that would be to risk a system conflict within myself," replied the Robot. "There is only a twenty-five-point-seven-percent chance of success. I cannot guarantee that I will survive. However, if it will save your family then I will gladly take the risk."

"I'll take the risk," came a gentle voice. It was GlimBus Two. "And that's a fact."

"It might work," said GlimBus the First. "If the Robot can download the System's database into GlimBus Two, then we may be able to return your family's memories to them. And, of course we would be able to keep the database here for our future use."

"But what if it doesn't work?" asked Penny.

"Then GlimBus Two will terminate," replied the alien.

"You mean he'll no longer function?" asked Penny. "We can't let that happen to GlimBus Two."

"But I *want* to do it," said GlimBus Two. "You helped me and now I want to help you. Isn't it a fact that that's what friends do? Help each other out of a 'jam,' as you call it?"

"By having GlimBus Two receive the data, the chances of success have increased to seventy-two-point-nine percent, Will Robinson," said the Robot.

"It appears you have little choice, young Robinson," said the older GlimBus.

Will knew instantly that GlimBus the First was right. "I guess it's seventy-two-point-nine percent or nothing," he agreed.

In a matter of minutes the Robot downloaded what was left of System Prime's database directly into GlimBus Two through the android's chestplate.

"I have now reactivated System Prime's command protocol," said GlimBus Two. "I am accessing the personality engrams of the humans. I am now transferring them to a disk."

Then GlimBus Two walked up to Professor Robinson. He opened the chestplate on the professor's chest and popped a newly transferred disk into a chamber inside. Professor Robinson's chestplate lit up. After a few minutes he blinked his eyes for the first time since Will had seen him in this condition. Then his chestplate went dark. As soon as it did GlimBus Two was able to remove the chestplate from Professor Robinson's chest.

"Wh — what happened?" asked Professor Robinson. "Where am I?"

"Dad!" Will and Penny exclaimed with happiness as they ran and hugged their father.

"Will? Penny?" their father asked groggily. "Are you all right?"

"We're fine!" said the children.

Suddenly Professor Robinson faltered with dizziness and fell to the ground, dazed.

"Do not worry, children," said GlimBus the First. "He is merely stunned from his experience. He will recover once he returns to the spaceship and rests."

One by one GlimBus Two freed the others from their trance-like state. They, too, were weak and groggy. Helped by the Dolians, Will and Penny brought their family, Don, and Dr. Smith back to the chariot, which was still parked in the plaza outside the Hall of Science. Only now it was surrounded by hordes of destroyed robots.

"Good-bye, GlimBus Two," said Will, when he was ready to leave. "And thanks."

"I am only sorry that there is no longer enough information in our computer library to help you return to your home world," said GlimBus Two.

"That's all right," said Will. "We've been doing pretty well so far. We'll get home one day, I'm sure of it."

"I wish I could be around to visit your world when you get there," said GlimBus Two.

"What do you mean?" asked Will. "Once we get back and tell people our story, a friendly ship from Earth will probably come here to meet your people. Especially now that GlimBus the First realizes how important it is to have contact with other planets."

"Yes," said GlimBus the First. "In order for any society to survive it must not fear the existence of others. Even with all our intelligence there is still much we can learn from another race."

"But, you don't understand, Will Robinson," GlimBus Two said sadly. "After you leave I will be turning myself over to the Dolians to be terminated. I am an imperfect android, a danger to this society. After all, all this was my fault. I was not able to prevent System Prime from taking over — "

"You must not blame yourself for what has happened on Dolia," GlimBus the First told the android. "It was I who created you. Any faults that are in your central brain stem from my own personal flaws."

"But I forgot to awaken you after five years, that's a fact!" insisted GlimBus Two. "If I had paid less attention to collecting facts and more attention to the general state of things then perhaps none of this would ever have happened."

"You are mistaken, little one," insisted GlimBus the First. "The mind engrams I implanted in you made you behave like a true Dolian. Curious, inquisitive, and scientific. No, little one. You will not be destroyed. I think you're perfect just the way you are."

"I think what he's saying is that he forgives you, GlimBus Two," Will told the android with a smile.

"Forgives — *me*?" asked GlimBus Two.

"Yes, I forgive you," agreed GlimBus the First. "In fact, I can't wait to have you help us when we begin to rebuild our library. We'll work side by side, like father and son."

"Oh, yes, yes." GlimBus Two smiled. "I would like that. There are so many facts to be discovered. To be *rediscovered*! And I promise I will never desire a mind of my own again. Your mind is my mind. Or is it the other way around?"

GlimBus the First laughed. "A mind of your own?" he asked. "Don't you see? If you *want* to have a mind of your own, that must mean you already have one. I think perhaps you always did."

"I did?" asked GlimBus Two with a smile. "I suppose I did! And that's a fact!"